Praise for SADIE-IN-WAITING by Annie Jones

"Jones beautifully conveys a range of emotions,
from the depth of despair to the pinnacle of joy...
readers will nod their heads with empathy toward
characters who seem like real people.
Throughout the novel, compassion and family bonds
bring hope, and God's love is shown to shine through
even the darkest of circumstances."
—*Romantic Times*

"Annie Jones writes about characters we all know and—
despite their quirks—love. Sadie Pickett is an endearing
character whose foibles and charms will leave you
smiling as you think, *Yes, life is just like that.* Carry on,
Sadie, and thanks for inviting us along for the ride!"
—Angela Hunt, author of *The Immortal*

"*Sadie-in-Waiting* is great mom lit...
those with teenagers and aging parents
will quickly relate to Sadie and her problems."
—*A Romance Review*

"*Sadie-in-Waiting* is full of funny one-liners
and sayings that will have you laughing.... Overworked
mothers of teenagers and daughters of aging parents
will see themselves in Sadie. More mom lit than
traditional romance, *Sadie-in-Waiting* is an enjoyable
read for a cold winter evening."
—*Romancejunkies.com*

A N N I E
J O N E S

Mom Over Miami

Happy Birthday,
Kathea

Annie Jones

Steeple
Hill
Café

Published by Steeple Hill Books™

STEEPLE HILL BOOKS

ISBN 0-373-78541-0

MOM OVER MIAMI

www.SteepleHill.com

Printed in U.S.A.

ACKNOWLEDGMENTS

No book ever made it from the author's hands
to the reader's without the hard work, dedication
and talent of many, many people.

I would like to thank some of those who helped
Mom Over Miami make that journey.

To the Princesses of Quite A Lot Prayer Group, Lynn,
Sharon and Diane. Each year and each new book I owe
you more and more. Thank you for being my safety net.

To my agent, Karen Solem, for believing I could write
"big" books and then helping me to make that happen.

To my children and all the years of research
they provided so I could write authentically
about a stressed-out mom.

To my husband, Bob, who took over driving duties when
I was behind in the book, behind in the laundry and just
couldn't climb back behind the wheel and trek to school
and beyond one more time. The little ways you show
support have always meant so much.

To Anna Cory-Watson for her patience e-mailing info
back and forth and answering my questions.

And to Joan Marlow Golan, who has believed in the
stories of Solomon's daughters and who planted the
seed of Hannah's story with a great suggestion,
and with her encouragement helped it grow.

Thank you.

1

Subject: Hannah's online at last!
To: ItsmeSadie, WeednReap
CC: SShelnutt, Phizziedigs
Hey, sisters (and Dad and Aunt Phiz)—
I finally got my computer up and running at the new house and couldn't wait to share some news and musings.

   Musings first. Remember how, starting back when I was five or six, every time Aunt Phiz got ready to leave after one of her visits I used to ask her to "pack me up and fly me away"? Well, I'm way too big to fit into any suitcase now, but I have to confess, y'all, some days around here, I sure do feel that powerful pull to just up and fly away!

I won't, of course. Not diligent, dependable old Hannah.

Not the woman who spent six years at various and sundry jobs to be the sole financial support of the Make Payton Bartlett a Pediatrician Fund.

Or the girl who invested three years of her life in college, majoring in journalism when clearly she never had it in her to realize that ambition.

Not me, who has given my all to countless well-intentioned, if hardly fruitful, home-extension classes in small-town haute cuisine, low-carb cookery and cake decorating for fun and profit. The last of which left me broken and blue—literally blue—from an ill-advised attempt to do an undersea landscape in frosting and food coloring.

I'm not going anywhere.

But tell me, after all that, what does it say about me that the thing that has finally made me "cool" among my foster son's pals is my ability to portion corn chips out of a warehouse-club monster bag, then drown said chips in pasteurized melted cheese product?

I'll tell you what it says. It says welcome to Nacho Mama's house.

Should have seen it coming when I got nominated as Snack Mom for Sam's soccer team. Moral: If a woman—wearing jewelry and cologne in the middle of the day, too-cute-to-walk-the-dog-in shoes, with a hairstyle that takes more than thirty-five seconds to maintain—offers you a large glass of iced tea at a team organizational meeting…run away. It's a trap.

Snack Mom.

It had all sounded so harmless at that first team meeting when Hannah had returned to the applause of the other moms who had managed to nominate, second, vote for and unanimously elect her while she had made a mad, iced-tea-induced dash to the ladies' room. All she'd have to do was buy in bulk and show up, right?

Ah. How young and foolish she'd been three weeks ago. That was before she'd learned that in the cutthroat arena of middle-class American child rearing, not all the competition remained on the soccer field.

School. Car pools. Extracurricular activities. Even church. All were littered with potential land mines of mommy-one-upmanship. And Hannah had stepped—no, been *thrown,* really—into the very center of it all.

Hannah Bartlett believed that Loveland, Ohio, was the friendliest town on the face of the earth. And living there was going to be the death of her.

Okay, *death* might be a bit strong.

But as she stood in the barely broken-in kitchen of her darling new house on this dank late-July afternoon, while a dozen eight-year-old boys who'd been rained out of soccer practice—again—played "quietly" in her unfurnished living room, the term "suffocating" *did* keep popping into her mind.

She would probably survive the experience of living in

the upscale-ish subdivision of this charming, convivial, quaint Ohio town. Perhaps she'd even grow stronger because of it. If she wasn't killed with kindness first.

Or smothered under the weight of her own powerlessness to tell nice people no.

Or stifled by her need to please and show everyone—i.e., her husband, and cutie pie extraordinaire, Dr. Payton Bartlett, M.D.; her older sisters, who still treated her like an inept, gullible child; and her much-adored daddy—that she could handle anything life threw at her.

Yes, *anything.* Even volunteering at her small—"small on the attendance rolls, large in the eyes of the Lord," as her new minister liked to admonish—church. And even learning the ropes of foster parenting Payt's eight-year-old distant cousin while mastering first-time motherhood at the age of thirty-six. Luckily, at six months, her daughter, Tessa, impressed easily. A game of peekaboo and a lullaby and the girl was eating out of Hannah's hand…well, or thereabouts.

And Sam, Hannah's foster son…

"You don't know anything." Sam bumped shoulders with the kid sitting next to him.

"Do so." The boy leapt up to tower over Sam.

Hannah held her breath.

"Nuh-uh," Sam shot back, his expression the sole province of prepubescent boys—something between a teenager's I-know-everything sneer and a kindergartner's you-are-a-big-dummy-head-and-I-don't-have-to-listen-to-you face.

Sam's combatant hunched his slender shoulders, obviously working up to a scathing, witty comeback. "Uh-huh," he said.

Hannah rolled her eyes and tried not to laugh.

Sam wrinkled his nose. His lips twitched.

"Hey, uh…" Hannah hated to single Sam out by only calling for him to knock it off without at least saying something to the other boy. Kyle, Hannah thought the kid's name was…or Cody. Colby? She glanced down at the enormous can of "American cheese food product" in her hands and a faint light flickered in the very back shelf of her memory. Cheddar? Gorgonzola?

Okay, neither of those were kids' names…probably. But since most of the adult conversations she'd had in the past week had taken place primarily in her head, she wasn't going to feel guilty about a few cheesy thoughts. She sighed, shoved the can under the blade of the electric can opener and opted for distraction over inconsequential discipline.

"Hey, Sam?" She kept her tone light. "Will you come help me a minute, please?"

He shot the other boy—whose name might be…Monterey Jack?—one last warning glance, then hurried around the half wall that divided the two rooms.

The can opener whirred under her hand for a good thirty seconds before clunking to a jarring stop.

Sam's rival melded into the knot of arms and legs and striped blue-and-white shirts with numbers on the back.

Hannah wrestled the can away from the opener.

"What can I do?" Sam leaned both elbows on the gleaming black granite countertop, though he had to stand on tiptoe to do it.

She stared at the big dent that had stopped the whirring blade cold. "Got any ideas for getting cheese out of a half-opened can?"

"If you melted it first, you could just pour it out."

"Great idea," she said, and was rewarded by a light in Sam's eyes that wasn't there as often as it should be. "Except…" She tapped one finger against the metal side.

"Oh."

"It won't microwave."

"And you don't know how to cook the regular way."

"Do so." Hey, eight-year-olds didn't own the patent on the brilliant retort.

"Yeah, but in the time it would take you to figure out how to melt that stuff inside the can…" He leaned back and looked at the dozen boys decked out in brand-spanking-new soccer regalia.

"The dog likes me best," one called.

Another elbowed his way to the front of the heap, vying for the attention of the family dog, a rescued racing greyhound with the affectionate and all-too-apt nickname Squirrelly Girl. "Only because you put your snack on the floor and she ate it."

"I'm going to put my snack on my head this time."

"I'm starving. I'm going to put my snack right in my stomach!"

"I see what you mean. If we don't feed them soon, it

may turn out like…" Hannah started to mention the grizzly story of that soccer team in the mountains turning to cannibalism, but caught herself in time. A reference to the novel *Lord of the Flies* also sprang to mind, followed by a flashback of her first PTA meeting. She shut her eyes and reminded herself to think like an eight-year-old boy now and use his frame of reference. "It might turn out like one of those reality TV survival shows."

"I know who I'd vote off first," Sam muttered.

"Let's hope it doesn't get to that." She held the can up and peered through the jagged slit already cut around the rim. "If only we could pry that back just enough to—"

"I got it!" Sam yanked open the junk drawer. He rummaged a moment and pulled out a huge screwdriver. Sam waved it around like he'd freed the sword Excalibur. "Old trusty!"

"Old trusty." Hannah smiled weakly at the offer. She had used that screwdriver to fish a pot holder out from behind the refrigerator. Before that, she'd used it to stab holes into the plastic covering of a microwavable lasagna. Before that, she'd even used the heavy wooden end of it to pound nails for hanging a picture.

"You got a better idea?"

"Fresh out." She sighed and took the tool from his hand. A lock of dark auburn hair fell over her eyes, which she ignored. She stuck out her tongue and pried the lid from the can with a screwdriver. At least none of the other mothers—the polished, poised, professional women who had caught her on a good day and immediately accepted her into their ranks—could see her now.

"There!" At last she scooped up an enormous mound of gelatinous cheeselike substance out of the can. It made a strangely satisfying *splat* landing in the big spouted mixing bowl she'd set out for the job. The aroma—and she was interpreting that term in the loosest possible sense here—filled the room. She popped the glop into the microwave.

Bleep-blip-beep-boop-boop.

Sam looked up at her, his mouth open as if awestruck by her astounding number-punching panache.

It was complex and crazy and corny as all get-out, but at that moment Hannah's whole being swelled with pride.

When her husband had broached the idea of providing a temporary home for Sam, Hannah had balked. The boy had been passed from family member to family member, his father denying any of them the chance of offering a permanent home through adoption. It sounded like a setup for heartbreak.

Sure, she'd wanted almost desperately to become a mother and, having "lost" her own mom as an infant, felt an instant affinity to any motherless child. But she knew nothing about little boys. The very thought of Sam had filled her with dread…and then she'd laid eyes on him.

Small for his age and scared, clutching a beat-up back-pack in both hands, he'd arrived with a set of plastic airline wings on his shirt and a quiver in his lower lip. Suddenly she couldn't imagine her life without him in it.

She hoped someday he would grow to trust, perhaps even love, her—if not as a mom then as a friend. It meant everything to her.

She brushed the fringe of brown hair out of his huge dark eyes and said, "It won't be much longer before it's ready. Do you want to call the boys in here now?"

He glanced over his shoulder to the living room with the plastic sheeting still covering the just-installed taupe-colored carpet.

Sam stubbed the toe of one shoe against the kickboard of the cabinet.

"Sam? I heard you talking to—" *Kraft? Velveeta?* "—your friend. Is there a problem?"

"Not really." He twisted his body around as if to head off to the next room, then dragged his foot, literally, to keep himself from making the short trip. "I just wondered…."

"What, Sam? If there's something bothering you, just let it out. I want you to feel like you can ask me anything."

He turned and fixed his anxious gaze right on her. "Are we poor?"

"What?" She flashed back to try to recall if she and Payt had argued about money recently and if the child could have overheard. But since their move to Ohio, where Payton came onboard with an established pediatrics practice, money had not been an issue.

Well, not one worth bickering about, anyway. In fact, for the first time in their marriage, Hannah had had the financial freedom to be a full-time stay-at-home mom. Of course, up until having her baby and bringing Sam into the fold she hadn't been *any* kind of mom, but the point still held.

"Honey, God has blessed us. Blessed us with health and a nice home and each other." She wanted to pull him into a hug but, mindful of the other boys, settled for giving his shoulder a squeeze. "Even if we didn't have a lot of money in the bank, 'poor' is not a word we would ever use to describe ourselves under any circumstances."

He nodded, but his lips twitched as though he wanted to say more.

"You want to tell me where you got an idea like that?"

He scratched the tip of his nose. "Stilton's mom."

"Stilton's mom?" *Stilton!* Of course! She stole a quick peek into the other room at the gangly boy who now had both arms wrapped around the greyhound's graceful neck. "*That's* Stilton?"

Hearing his name, the boy looked up and blinked at her from behind faux tortoiseshell-rimmed glasses.

She smiled and gave a stiff, awkward wave to the child. "Hi, Stilton. I really got a lot out of talking to your mom at the meeting the other day."

"Uh, okay." He nodded, then fixed his attention on the dog again, stroking the silky white spot on the animal's broad chest.

"Hmm." Hannah shook her head. Somehow she'd expected Stilton to be…different. Gorgeous and gifted. Maybe even slightly glowing. At least that's what she had envisioned based on his mother's descriptions of him at the parents' meetings.

If Hannah were a superhero in the cartoon comic strip of her life, her archnemesis would be represented by one faux-tanned, French-manicured, fabulously coiffed package of plastic-surgeon's-trophy-wife perfection—Stilton's mom. The woman was…

"Stilton said she told him not to tease me about our not having any living room furniture because maybe we're house poor, and if we are or not, it's none of his business so don't go pointing it out."

Actually, Stilton's mom was very nice.

That only made Hannah feel all the more inferior to her. Inferior and rotten for her lapses into petty jealousy. "Well, don't worry about it, Sam. We'll have furniture in the front room…someday."

"When the store finds our order, right?"

She smiled. "Right."

"Because somewhere in a warehouse in Pakquipsee there's a footstool with our name on it."

"You sound just like Payt."

The boy grinned at the comparison to the latest in a long line of father figures he'd known in his young life.

The sight both warmed and wounded Hannah's heart. "The topping is ready. Go tell the team to come and get it."

He started off.

"Oh, and put 'Squirrel' out, so we don't have a repeat of last time." Hannah pulled up a stack of disposable bowls from the towering package she'd gotten at the warehouse club, dropped a handful of greasy corn chips into it and stood there waiting for the onslaught.

A dozen eight-year-old boys stumbled and pushed each other, trying to be first in line, and Hannah knew why.

"Mrs. Bartlett, is this snack homemade?" A black-haired boy with skin the color of dark chocolate took the bowl from her hand. He raised it up until it hid his grin, and just his brown eyes peered over the rim. "Because the snacks are always homemade at *my* mama's house."

She drizzled the melted cheese concoction over the boy's chips. She knew what he wanted her to say in her distinct central Kentucky accent, but she just didn't think she had the energy to play the game today. "Hunter, honey, I'm afraid our cheese-making equipment and smooth stones for pounding cornmeal into chips are not unpacked yet, so I couldn't make any of this at home."

"But at *my* mama's house…"

Hannah raised her head. "Next."

"Mrs. Bartlett!" The boy shifted from one foot to the other. "At *my* mama's house…"

"Mine, too," the next boy said, cupping the bowl she'd given him in both hands.

"Everything is homemade at *my* mama's house, too, Mrs. Bartlett," Third-in-line chimed in.

They were not going to give up until she gave them what they wanted.

"At *my* mama's house…" Hunter started again.

"At *my* mama's house, at *my* mama's house…" She mimicked the boys with a swagger in her shoulders. Giving them the show she knew they wanted, she plunked her hand on her hip and narrowed one eye. "That may all be well and good, but let me tell you something, boys, this is *not* your mama's house—"

"Nacho Mama's house!" Hunter laughed. "I got her to say it."

"Yes, you did, Hunter. You got me good." She poured a thin thread of liquefied cheese onto the next serving of chips and wondered what had happened to her big plans of living the sophisticated and intellectually stimulating life of a lady of leisure?

Hannah looked out over the heads of the boys, and her gaze met Sam's. *That's* what had happened. Sam had happened.

And to a lesser extent Tessa who, even though she wasn't as demanding as an eight-year-old *now*, thank the Lord…

As if Tessa had a direct line into Hannah's thoughts, and had inherited the Shelnutt family knack for usually proving those thoughts wrong, the baby sleeping in the nursery down the hall let out a sudden, toe-curling wail.

"Nacho Mama! Nacho Mama!" The boys who had been served lifted their bowls over their heads and chanted as they snaked their way back to the plastic-protected living room.

Tessa wailed.

Hannah dipped up another serving and then another as fast as she could.

"Nacho Mama! Nacho Mama!" More boys joined the chorus.

Stilton stepped up in line.

Hannah picked up a bowl and flung a few chips into it.

"No, thank you." Stilton shook his head, one eye squinted at her like he might examine a bug before he decided whether to squash it or set it free. "I'm lactose intolerant."

Cheese boy, lactose intolerant? Hannah didn't know whether to smile at the notion or marvel at the boy's maturity. "Can I get you something else then, Stilton?"

"No, thank you." After a moment of studying her, he leaned in, tilted his head and whispered, "Do you need some help, Mrs. Bartlett?"

She had a cranky baby down the hall, a mixing bowl of blistering hot cheese stuff that she dared not leave unattended in her kitchen, and a soccer team dancing the Nacho Mama mambo in her living room. And the kid wanted to know if she needed help?

Stilton's mom would not need help. She'd handle the boys, the baby, the bedlam and probably bake a homemade Bundtcake to boot! Hannah, on the other hand…

She'd never admit this to another soul, but seeing as it was a sober-faced child who'd already had a sense of pity for Hannah and her family instilled in him, she broke down and confessed, "Actually, Stilton, I *do* need help. In fact, some people might take one look at this situation and say I need divine intervention."

What she got…was a phone call.

2

Subject: P.S.
To: ItsmeSadie, WeednReap
CC: SShelnutt, Phizziedigs
Hey, there—
P.S.—which in this case stands for "Pressed Send." As in I pressed send on that last note too soon. Wanted to make sure I didn't give the impression that I've bitten off more than I can chew with this Snack Mom business.

Pun intended, of course.

I'm a writer, even if all I manage to write is soccer team flyers, church nursery schedules and corny e-mails. At least I studied to be a writer and still hope to be one—someday.

Anyway, just wanted to emphasize that if I pepper

my posts with bad puns, or flavor the simple stories about everyday life around here with both the sweet and the sour, those reflect my dream of being a writer more than my inadequacies at…pretty much everything else.

Love,

Hannah, girl writer

Subject: Addendum to P.S.

To: ItsmeSadie, WeednReap

Okay, sisters dear, I have issues. I know it. So I want the people I care about to think I'm at least competent enough to feed cheese and chips to the league's losing-est ever soccer team. Don't send me links to Web sites about improving self-esteem. Don't offer me tips on how to be a better mom, cook or writer.

I love you both with all my heart.

Now leave me alone.

The ringing phone rattled her down to her very last nerve.

She clenched her jaw. She shut her eyes. She stuck her hand out to avoid mowing down in her rush the perfect—with the possible exception of a little lactose intolerance—child of Loveland's most perfect mom. "Excuse me, Stilton, but…"

But the boy had fled. He now stood huddled in the corner of the living room with his hands over his ears.

For one fleeting moment, Hannah thought about joining him.

R-r-r-r-ring!

The sound jangled her back to her harried reality.

"Please be Payt saying he's done at work and is so close by, he can get here in seconds to pitch in," she whispered in prayer even as she lunged for the phone. "Hello?"

"Hannah-Banana! It's your favorite aunt."

Phyllis Amaryllis Shelnutt Shaffer Wentz, her father's twice-widowed only sister. If Hannah had had a dozen aunts, the one they always called "Phiz" (though no one could ever remember why) would still have been her favorite.

That didn't mean she was always a welcome interruption.

"Hi, Aunt Phiz. You sort of caught me in the middle of something." Hannah elected not to share the details. Compared to her aunt's amazing adventures, a little cheesy chaos hardly merited mention.

"Did I catch you at a bad time?" Phiz hollered back, clearly having not heard her niece say almost that very thing.

"Yes! It's not the best time to take a call."

Unless, of course, the now-retired college professor, part-time archaeologist and full-time family meddler had called to say she was in the neighborhood. And that she would be glad to drop in and save the day—or whisk Hannah away from it all.

"Can you hear me, dear? You have to excuse the poor connection, as I'm halfway around the world—in China!"

"'Peace. Be strong,'" Hannah muttered the verse from Daniel that her father had chosen as her personal axiom in childhood.

"What, dear?"

"Nothing Aunt Phiz. You just caught me at a bad time." She said the last part louder, hoping against hope it would sink in with her aunt at last.

But the boys' voices rose in the background and drowned her out even in her own ears.

Tessa's cry had turned into a soggy-sounding cough.

The dog pressed her entire lean muscled body against the sliding glass window. She gave out a mournful high-pitched whine begging to be let inside, and Stilton—who probably thought this qualified as helping—obliged.

Every other boy in the living room leapt up, bowls of food held above their heads.

Over the uproar, Aunt Phiz shouted, "What's that, dear? I didn't catch you at a bad time, did I?"

Hannah considered using the receiver like a hammer and pounding it against her forehead; instead, she trapped it between her head and shoulder and got to work. First, she kicked the fridge door open with the toe of her shoe, then kept it from closing again with a well-timed swing of her hip. "I have Sam's soccer team here, and Tessa seems to be getting a cold and I need to take her a juice bottle."

"Then take me along with you. I assume you're on a cordless?"

Hannah pushed aside juice boxes and milk jugs to retrieve the prepared bottle. "Yes, I'm on the cordless but…"

"Good. I'll tag along and goo for the baby in Cantonese. The tour group is celebrating our departure for India tonight, and I don't know when I'll get near a phone again."

Hannah sighed and braced the phone wedged against her shoulder in place with her "free" hand. "If there's a celebration, maybe you should get back to it, Aunt Phiz."

She could just picture the tall, robust woman leading a wildly energetic dragon dance—the locals laughing and chanting as they wound this way and that behind her. "Hey, that could work."

"Of course it will work, just take the phone with you and—"

"Grab your nachos with both hands, boys, and get in line. We're snake-dancing all the way to the baby's room."

Even as the boys hurried to get a spot in line and still keep their bowls above greyhound-head height, someone called, "We never do stuff like this at *my* mama's house,"

"I told you before, this is not your mama's house."

"Nacho Mama's house!" The boys laughed and wriggled behind her down the hallway.

Aunt Phiz gave a quick rundown of the time she expected to arrive in Cincinnati two weeks hence.

Hannah made it to the crib. She scooped her daughter up. Somehow she managed to cradle the phone against the child's ear while getting the bottle into Tessa's mouth *and* steering the soccer team back into the hallway with only a couple chip spills—which Squirrel happily lapped up.

Everyone was being fed.

Everyone was happy.

Hannah sighed. Maybe she was getting a handle on this motherhood thing after all.

"Oops!" The phone slid out from under Tessa's warm pink cheek.

Aunt Phiz, her unfamiliar dialect sounding to Hannah like a cartoon watch spring breaking, kept right on babbling in Cantonese baby talk.

Hannah came to a full stop to catch the phone. Only after she did that did she realize the consequences.

Th-whap!

Thud.

Crunch.

"Ouch."

Then a momentary silence before:

"Hey, the dog is licking the back of my head."

"That's because it's got cheese on it."

"Cheesehead! Cheesehead!"

"Boys, boys!" Hannah spun around to find melted cheese product stuck in hair, all over shirts and even on the dog. Crushed chips littered the floor. One kid had stepped in his dropped bowl and had it stuck to his shoe.

Unsure which disaster to tackle first, Hannah ordered, "Nobody move!"

Tessa heaved the bottle to the floor.

Squirrel cowered.

"Okay, change of plan. *Move.* Everybody into the kitchen!"

The boys started to do as she said, but about that time the dog, who was crouching at the back of the line, noticed the bounty of chips on the plastic floor covering. Just as the group did as Hannah had asked, sixty-two pounds of long, strong, determined greyhound decided to begin belly-walking between the boys' feet.

The few bowls that had not fallen to the floor were goners, and so were the boys holding those bowls.

Down in a pile they all went like…like…like a load of broken chips poured from God's greatest corn chip bag.

Hannah groaned.

Then the doorbell rang.

"Oh, great." She checked the clock. Still too early for parental pickups.

At least *that* was on her side.

She could deal with the door, get the boys cleaned up, tend to Tessa and pull up the ruined plastic drop cloth before any of the other mothers saw what a big fat failure she was at handling even the most simple of mommy duties.

"Bye, Aunt Phiz, I've got to go," Hannah hollered at the receiver lying on the floor.

Aunt Phiz, never missing a beat, went right on chattering in Chinese.

"Hang that up, Sam," Hannah said as she hoisted Tessa on her hip and headed for the door.

Whatever they were selling or soliciting donations for, she would get rid of the caller, then get this household back under control. She had three years of college journalism under her belt. She had lived with a nutty father in a small-town fishbowl. She had even recently survived discovering that the mother she had lived a lifetime hoping to find had died not long after the family broke up. Hannah had run a rural pediatric clinic. She had overcome disappointment and infertility, begun motherhood at an age when a lot of women were done with that sort of thing, and still managed to meet the standards of the Foster Parent program.

Hannah could handle anything.

She flung open the door. "I'm sorry but…"

The boys crowded forward around her, pressing cheese-smeared hands to the doorjamb and Hannah's jeans.

Amend that. Hannah could handle anything except…

Stilton slid under her arm and beamed up at her. "When you said you needed divine in-inner…intention, I knew just what to do, Mrs. Bartlett."

"Why…" Hannah's shoulders slumped. Her heart sank. The corners of her mouth tightened into a smile as she strained a pleasant tone though clenched teeth, "Thank you, Stilton, but you shouldn't have. *Really*."

"Oh, no trouble," her guest gushed. "That's why we got Stilton a cell phone—so he could use it in case of emergency."

Hannah forced a weak, empty laugh. "Emergency? Oh, this hardly qualifies as an—"

One of the boys shoved the phone toward Hannah.

"I don't know what this guy's problem is, Mrs. B." A man's voice, probably one of Aunt Phiz's fellow travelers, blasted out through the receiver a Cantonese cootchie-coo.

The dog rolled over on her back, rubbing greasy orange cheese residue on two boys' new soccer shoes at once.

And Tessa sneezed, spewing bright red juice directly into the face of none other than Lauren Faison—aka Stilton's mom.

"Oh, who am I trying to kid?" Hannah motioned the world's most perfect mom into the chaos of her home and said, "Come on in, and heaven help us all."

3

Subject: Good News/Bad News
To: ItsmeSadie, WeednReap
CC: Phizziedigs
Hi, there y'all—
The good news: They've found our furniture!

The bad news: I think I've lost my mind.

What other explanation can there be for Payt and me standing at our back door just after dawn on Saturday, wadding up sliced cold cuts into little ham and salami bombs and lobbing them into the garage to lure Squirrelly Girl in there? You know, that dog might not be quick on the uptake, but as a greyhound she's not slow. That's one thing she had over us in our scheme to get her in the garage then hit the door opener—in this case, door closer—and trap her safely inside. We'd no sooner land a lump of deli meat on the garage floor and hit the button when she'd gobble it down, race out to the driveway and look at us standing in the half-open door with an expression on her dopey adorable doggie face that said "Hey, y'all should come out here. It's raining ham!"

So we'd load up and try again. We must have stayed at it for a good half an hour before we finally left her outside and let the chips—and I don't mean nachos—fall where they may.

In our defense, it did seem like a really brilliant idea at the time.

—Hannah, skunk-sprayed dog owner

Sam staggered sleepily into the living room and pinched his nose. His voice sounded like a cartoon character with a cold when he asked, "What stinks?"

"The dog." Hannah held their fawn-colored greyhound's bright pink leash out as far as her arm would allow. Once they'd cornered Squirrelly Girl they hadn't dared let her run off and hide—or worse, have another run-in with her new stinky play pal.

The boy grimaced and maneuvered around to keep from getting on the tail end of the beast. "What'ja feed her? Rotten eggs?"

"It's not coming *from* her." Hannah laughed. "She had a run-in with a skunk."

"A skunk?" He looked around but wisely did not take his fingers from his nose. "Where?"

"It was under the back deck." She pointed to the ground-level redwood decking jutting out from the sliding glass doors at the back of the living room. "We tried to get the dog into the garage, but—"

Hannah stopped. The kid thought he was living with two bright, capable, clear-thinking individuals at last. Why shake his faith with the retelling of the ham-bomb story?

"But we couldn't get the dog to stay in the garage, so Payt ran off to the grocery store to get some tomato juice."

"Huh?"

"Hmm, guess that made about as much sense as saying, 'I lost my shoe so I ate a sandwich,' huh?"

"You lost your shoe?" Sam looked down at the fuzzy pink slippers on her feet.

"No, it was a non sequitur."

"I thought you said it was a sandwich?" He looked decidedly worried.

"No, the sandwich is just a…" She tried to think how to explain the concept in terms Sam would get right away.

Before her brain would engage, though, the dog, spotting the only human in the house likely to be on her side in the whole "what's a little stink when you're having fun?" issue, lurched for Sam.

Jerked forward, Hannah fought to stand her ground. That was all she wanted at this point, wasn't it?

In her family life and in her relationships and responsibilities? *To simply stand her ground.*

And maybe not get skunk smell on her house shoes.

She reined in the dog and smiled at Sam. "Forget the sandwich, honey. Payt went to get the tomato juice so we can bathe the dog in it."

Sam's expression went from worried to bewildered.

"The juice gets the smell out." She struggled to keep Squirrelly still, which was about as easy as trying to hold a kite motionless on a windy day. "Or at least that's what Aunt April said when I called her for advice."

"You're going to give Squirrelly Girl a bath in *tomato juice?*"

"We're going to try."

"*This* I want to see!"

Hannah glanced down at the lean, muscular animal and winced. "Oh, don't worry. I'm counting on you to help."

"I like to help." Sam grinned. "In fact, I wish you'd waked me up so we could have all gone to the grocery store together!"

"I almost did, but then…" But then she'd come to her senses.

They'd chosen Loveland and this particular subdivision in the town for the closeness to schools, shopping and church. They could find all of those things within a few blocks of the house. This helped them "create the ambience of community while still enjoying the larger context of the city setting." At least that's what the Realtor had told them.

And it had sounded grand at the time. After all, Hannah and Payt had grown up in a small town with its own unique "ambience." They had returned to that town for

Payt to put in his years as an intern and a resident. They liked community.

Up to a point.

Hannah, at least, liked it in theory. And in the way it made her feel safe and not cast adrift in the unknown territory of her new life. And that it made the world a cozier place to raise her children, but…

But they'd moved to Ohio hoping to escape some of the very things close proximity to everyone provided. She hated thinking that the people across the street might call out to her some Monday morning, "Hey, we didn't see you in church yesterday, is someone sick? Should I bring over a casserole?"

She could do without that, thank you very much. Well, except for the casserole. *That* she—and those fated to eat her cooking—might actually appreciate.

But the idea of living so totally exposed and available? Hannah shivered. Would it mean that any given evening, as she snuggled up to her hubby on the couch in the few moments of private time they managed to snatch out of the day, a knock could come at the door and the head of the PTA could be standing there with a box of envelopes that needed stuffing? "Hi. No one showed up for my committee this afternoon, but I saw your lights on and knew you wouldn't mind contributing a little of your time."

Her shiver transformed into a shudder.

"Honestly, Sam, honey, I didn't wake you up because I can't go anywhere around here without running into someone I know." That meant she always left the house primped, pressed, armed with a repertoire of small talk. And ready with a list of polite and reasonable excuses for not being able to stop and indulge in any talking—small or otherwise. "I never set foot outside this house without looking fresh and fabulous. Even if I just need to run out for a case of tomato juice to de-skunk the dog."

Hannah lifted the leash, and the dog responded by spinning around and sending the odor wafting out in all directions.

"Ugh." Sam wrinkled up his nose.

Hannah spun counter to the dog to keep the poor thing from making things worse by adding getting tangled in her own leash to an already-trying morning. In doing that, Hannah caught a glimpse of herself in the sliding-glass door. "Make that a double ugh."

She yanked first at one, then the other, of short, frayed braids sticking out from either side of her head, trying to even them out a bit. It didn't help. "Guess you can see why I couldn't just roust you and Tessa out of bed and go along with Payt, not with me looking like Pippi Longstocking on a bad hair day."

"Pippi *who?*"

"Never mind. The important thing is—"

"The important thing is that we're the best hiders in the whole neighborhood?" Sam beamed up at her.

"Hider?" Her pulse did a quick jig. "Sam, I'm not trying to hide from anyone." Well, not *exactly*. "It's more a case of…"

He tipped his head up, his mouth open and his nose still pinched closed.

How could she explain to that sweet face that she sometimes felt so insecure about herself that she'd let people talk her into doing way more than she should ever even attempt? She couldn't—not without planting a seed in his mind that she only agreed to take him into her home out of guilt, and the driving desire to please people and show everyone how much she was needed. Of course, at eight he wouldn't have the sophistication to put it in that framework. But being a kid in the foster system, he'd pick up on the nuances on a gut level.

Hannah knew. She'd grown up as that kid from the less-than-normal household. She understood how a child might take a seemingly innocent remark and bury it in his or her heart. Where no one would know it lay hidden. But the child would know. The child would keep those words deep inside for always, and they might affect how that child grew up—who that child eventually became.

The very story of her own life had begun with her mother abandoning their family. In telling about it, her father always added, "And with Hannah just three weeks home from the hospital."

Growing up with that ingrained in her makeup, what could any human being ever say or do to make her feel truly loved and wanted?

They would try, of course. And on an intellectual level, she accepted their assertions. On the surface of things, she'd moved along with cool ease and confidence because up there—on that surface—she realized that everything in her life looked pretty great.

To whine or complain about pretty much anything would seem shallow and petty. And since she lived her life always trying to make sure she never gave anyone any more reasons to reject her, shallowness and pettiness were qualities she could not afford. So she'd put her best foot forward. Her best shoes, best clothes, best hair and—always, always, always—best smile. Since it was all she knew she could rely on, she kept a tight rein on *that* tidy veneer.

But deep down, hidden in the dark pockets of her soul, she'd always carried a very real fear.

If her own mother didn't want her, then who could?

And because she was a flawed being, she would find plenty of reasons why no one would choose her as a daughter, sister, friend, wife or mother. So she would—perhaps without always realizing she was doing it—go for the next best thing.

Maybe people couldn't fully love her, but if she worked hard enough, if she acted sweet enough, if she gave and gave and gave and did not ask for much in return, then maybe people would at least begin to *need* her.

If Hannah was anything, she was needed. So much so that she couldn't do something as simple as take the family out of the skunk-scented house long enough for a morning run to the grocery store for fear someone would nab her for a favor. Or worse, see her shortcomings and decide she wasn't needed at all.

But how could she explain all that complex stuff, much of which she had barely worked out herself, to a child that she wanted more than anything to protect from those very demons?

"Okay. I'm hiding. But just a little bit." She held her thumb and forefinger a fraction of an inch apart and peered at him through the opening. "You see, there are these two sisters. You remember them. The ones that have their own interior design business and told you they'd like to decorate your room for you as a welcome present?"

"The ones that smell like paint and flap their hands when they talk?"

"Uh-huh."

"And they talk *all* the time?"

"That would be them." She shut her eyes a moment. Maybe now Sam would cut her some slack about not wanting to go out this morning and risk seeing them. "Anyway, these ladies—they want me to volunteer at church…"

"Church?" He raised his eyebrows and finally let go of his nose. "You're hiding from church ladies?"

"Well…" She held her thumb and forefinger up again to illustrate the minuteness of her sin. Then quickly she moved all her fingers in counterpoint to her thumb, the universal sign for someone yakking her head off, just to remind Sam of who it was she was avoiding.

"B-but—" he shook his head "—you can't hide from God."

"No! No, I wouldn't. That is, I never intended to…" Or had she? For weeks now she'd dodged the two women that everyone called the DIY sisters and their repeated attempts to enlist her help. "But I just don't see how I could take on any more responsibilities."

"Not even for God?"

"It isn't exactly for God, Sam. It's for the nursery."

He folded his arms, his head bobbling with eight-year-old attitude. "At *church*."

Oh, he was go…o…o…d.

Sighing, Hannah ruffled her fingers through her hair until a stray red strand fell over her forehead. She gritted her teeth and forced out a sigh. "Fine. If God asks, then okay. I'm Mrs. Available."

Not too risky of a promise seeing as they were ensconced safely at home this morning.

"In the meantime, let's take Squirrel outside and let her air out a bit."

"Yeah. Let's get out of here." He dashed toward the back door.

"No, Sam! Better take her out front—if we let her out back, she'll just roll in the scent again."

"She's not very smart, is she?" He made a quick detour and launched himself ahead of Hannah and the dog.

"Well, as my Daddy used to say, 'If brains were baking powder, that poor thing wouldn't have enough to bake herself a biscuit.'"

"I like your daddy. He makes me laugh." Sam yanked the door inward.

"Oh, yeah, my daddy is more fun than a barrel of—"

"Church ladies!" Sam grinned up at the two women standing framed in Hannah's front door.

"Oh, Hannah! You're home!" Cydney Snowden, the more…retiring—if you could call wearing handmade clothing covered with your own artwork and plastic jewels retiring—of the pair of sisters threw her hands up.

"We saw your car leaving as we turned the corner and thought you'd be gone." Jacqui Lafferty, definitely the dominant diva, cocked her head and narrowed just one eye, sizing Hannah up.

Cydney pushed forward, a sour-apple-green piece of paper in her hand. "So we've been sitting in your drive trying to fit everything we have to say onto one of our business cards!"

Hannah took the card and glanced at the front of it. "The DIY-Namic Duo. Isn't that…cute?"

She did not flip the card over to read the message telling her what they had wanted. Hannah knew what they wanted.

And she had just promised Sam that she'd give it to them.

4

Subject: What have I done?
To: ItsmeSadie
Hi, Sadie—
Do unto others as you would have them do unto you.
Simple, huh? The Golden Rule. Something we should
all aspire to, right?

I thought so myself until it happened to me. Yes, I've
been done unto—by a pair of first-class do-it-yourself-
ers. Literally. They call themselves the DIY sisters and
they are a handful. Two handfuls? I don't know. What
I do know is that Jacqui Lafferty and Cydney Snowden have enough energy to tackle anything—and anyone! And there I was Saturday morning, standing in
the proverbial end zone, with nothing more substan-

tial to protect me than my fuzzy slippers and my desire to set a good example for Sam.

"Oh, no," they said, rushing into my house—did I tell you we still don't have any furniture and the house smells like we're stewing skunk in tomato soup? Anyway, they worm their way into my house, assuring me they only want me to pitch in as I can. "We wouldn't dream of asking you to take on the whole nursery program yourself. We haven't had an official program director in over a year and we've done all right."

Picture, if you will, a sad, big-eyed puppy saying this—one with flecks of paint in her perky blond hair standing next to an even bigger-eyed puppy wearing a slightly askew vest that she quilted with her own two hands.

They were so sweet. So earnest. So undemanding.

That's how they get you.

Confused? Welcome to my world!

The upshot of it all is that I have stepped forward—pushed, actually, but in such a nice way I couldn't decline—and volunteered to take on running the church nursery program.

There are a few little "issues" of concern. Jacqui made little quote marks in the air as she told me this to clue me in that these "issues" are neither little nor are there only a few. Apparently the Sunday school teachers and those who help out during the services have been, um, pulling rank on the lowly nursery workers. So in hopes of reminding everyone that we are all doing the Lord's work, I made us this sign to post.

In many ways we feed the flock,
They also serve who sit and rock.

Cute? Too cute? Cowardly? Maybe I should adapt it and do a drawing of myself as a big chicken—they also serve who sit and cluck!
Your fine-feathered sister

"You are so cute." Payton strolled into the almost-bare nursery with a stack of mail under his arm.

"No. *You* are," Hannah insisted, looking up at her darling hubby with his close-cropped sandy hair, white shirt and black tie, slightly askew. Yum. Even after all these years of marriage, he still sent a thrill through her. She wriggled in the tiny red plastic chair pushed against the low, round table she'd dragged from the basement to the shabby room she planned to use for the toddlers. "What'cha got there?"

"Oh, just some mail forwarded to my office."

"Didn't you fill out those postal forms to give them our new home address yet?"

"I'm right on top of it." He plopped down some envelopes and last week's copy of the *Wileyville Guardian News* then gave her a wink.

She sighed and shook her head. "Do you want me to—"

"That'd be great." He hitched up his pants and made a point of giving their surroundings the once-over. "Look at this place. You've only been here a couple hours, and you've got it all whipped into shape."

"I've been here *four* hours, and feel like I've been whipped."

When she'd arrived this morning, she found the room connected to the baby nursery stuffed to overflowing with moldering file boxes, half-empty paint cans and a tower of carpet samples from the seventies. After a morning of lifting and lugging and heaving and hauling, it finally bore some resemblance to a workable playroom for the post-potty-training set. Most women would celebrate that small accomplishment with pride and be done with it.

"I'm starting to make some headway," she conceded. "But it's going to take at least another weekend's work before I can put kids in here in good conscience."

"Looks fine to me."

"Yes, but you're hardly an expert, are you?"

"Yeah, all those years in the study of pediatrics, what could I possibly have picked up?" He laughed.

"I just want everything to be…"

"Perfect."

She pursed her lips.

"Perfection is God's department, honey. No matter how hard you try or how badly you want it, you are not going to muscle in on His territory. We grubby little humans just do the best we can. And you have. You have worked a minor miracle here today."

"Miracle? That's a bit strong. But thank you." She let her palm glide over the cool, slick surface of the table that brushed against her knee.

"You really are something," he murmured.

"No, you *are*." And she meant that.

Payt Bartlett was average looking, not a classically handsome man, though by all rights he should have been. In fact, if pressed for a word to describe his particular kind of attractiveness, *handsome* was the word most people used, but always with a decided hesitation.

He was born into small-town Southern aristocracy, the youngest son of a monied family. Deal makers every last son and daughter—except Payt. People expected him to be handsome—and charming—and successful in all he put his hand to. That was the expectation. The reality?

He scratched under his chin, then rubbed one knuckle over the dark circle under his eye. "I would never have stuck with this project long enough to get this much done."

The reality—Payt spoke the absolute truth. Finishing what he started? Not the man's strong suit. To begin with, Payt had the organizational skills of a mud wasp. Provided, of course, that mud wasps' organizational skills rate a zero.

He stifled a yawn and slid his hands into the deep pockets of his gray trousers. "Do you still need me to pick up the kids and take them home, or are you all done here?"

"You aren't trying to wriggle out of taking the kids for a while, are you?"

"Nope." He moved toward her and lifted her chin up with one crooked finger. "I have no problem taking care of the kids for an afternoon, for a whole day—hey, a whole week—if you'd ever allow that to happen."

A week? Just hearing it made her stomach clench. "What are you saying?"

"I'm saying we could get along just fine without you."

Hannah's cheeks burned. Her eyes grew moist. She hardly had breath enough to force out a meek little "Oh."

"Not that we'd ever *want* to." Her husband took both her hands and pulled her to her feet. "But if push came to shove, I could keep the kids alive until you could come and set the whole world right again."

She put her forehead to his and let her anxiety ease away with a laugh.

"So, you want to take the big gamble and let me watch the kids for the afternoon?"

"Actually, no."

He opened his mouth, but she pressed two fingers to his lips to stop him from arguing or teasing her or whatever he had planned in his warped little mind.

"Tessa is asleep in the baby room, and Sam is doing something for me in there, too. So…"

"So you've got everything under control."

His words, not hers.

She smiled. "No need for you to stick around. In fact, if you really want to be a big help to me, why don't you go on home and start lunch? We'll be along in a half hour or so."

"Lunch. Got it." He kissed her cheek, turned to go, then faced her again, his brow creased. "What should I make?"

She ran her fingers back through her hair to try to work out a little of the tension in her scalp. "You worked as a short-order cook for a little while—surprise me."

His mouth tilted up on one side. "Surprising people was why I only worked as a cook for a little while."

"Don't start with that old story about growing up a poor little rich boy who never did anything right."

"You left out 'according to your dad.'"

"Oh, right—who, according to your dad, never did anything right. And so you never had the drive and desire to stick with anything."

"Not the military school, not the Coast Guard, not publishing, not college."

"Well, maybe not the first time you went, but—"

"But by the time I finally got it together, dear old Dad had had enough." He smiled, sort of. "Can't say I blame him."

Hannah blamed him. Oh, not for finally refusing to fund what, at the time, must have seemed Payton's never-ending quest for fulfillment, but for washing his hands entirely of his son. It cut Payt to his very core. It had to. And yet he never mentioned it as anything but a joke.

But Hannah knew. She knew those secret aches that never wholly healed, and she saw how having disappointed his father still gnawed at Payt. She saw it in the flicker in his eyes whenever he talked about the family who'd disowned him despite all he had become. She saw it in the way her husband strove to impress the older male authority figures in his life, often at great cost to himself and those he loved.

That was why Payt had gone in to work this Saturday morning, to catch up on signing forms and returning calls and going over the details of the everyday running of the office that his boss chose to ignore. Payt wanted to show the man that he had the makings of a great doctor. And Payt's boss probably would never even notice. The work got done. He didn't care how or by whom.

Hannah had wanted to point that very thing out to Payt. The ultimate example of the pot calling the kettle black, she decided, so she kept her mouth shut.

"That's how the story goes, isn't it?" She placed her hand just below her throat and raised her chin to supply the proper theatrics. "The Payton-Bartlett story of youthful debauchery and eventual self-discovery? You couldn't fully commit yourself to anything until you found the Lord and your calling as a doctor."

"I never could commit to anything until I found the Lord and *you*, Hannah."

Her heart swelled with love for this man. Her man. She bit her lip to keep from standing there surrounded by two-foot-high furniture and grinning like a fool. She had loved this man from the day she met him and saw in him things no one else could ever appreciate.

Of course, with that love came awesome responsibilities. One of which was to keep the man honest and on his toes.

"Oh, please." She shook her head, smiling slyly. "You had decided to become a doctor before we ever met, Bartlett."

He grinned to hear her address him the way she had when they first met, when she thought of him as some spoiled rich kid who could do with being taken down a peg or two.

"In fact—" she put her finger to her chin to feign dredging up the memories from some dusty corner of her mind "—I believe you were on a mission trip trying to impress another girl when you realized you had a calling to enter med school."

"Okay, I had decided to study medicine before we met, but, baby, I wouldn't be where I am today without you."

"Don't I know it." She added an impromptu head swagger. "*Baby.*"

"Wow! That's the first time I ever remember you accepting that compliment."

"What compliment?" She batted her eyes and went to him, placing both her palms flat on his chest. "I'm saying that without me, you'd never be standing in a poorly lit, dreary-walled, carpeted-with-stuff-I-wouldn't-put-in-a-dog's-house, makeshift church nursery. You can thank me later."

"I can thank you now." He kissed her, briefly but hard. "*And* I can thank you later."

She returned his kiss with one of her own, lighter and tinged with an unexpected giggle. "Why don't you start by thanking me with lunch?"

"I don't know what to make."

"Then stop and pick up some chicken or burgers."

"Chicken or burgers? Too much pressure. Why don't I wait until you're done and we'll all go out together?"

Payt spoke no lie when he said he'd never have become a doctor without her. She loved the man, but that didn't blind her to the fact that he lacked direction. And motivation. And sometimes needed a swift kick in the seat of the pants.

"Payton. You are my inspiration. The light of my life. You are the only man I could ever imagine trusting my heart, my home, my children to. I am so privileged to have you to spend the rest of my life with…." She smiled and knew that no way could that smile contain all the love and admiration she felt for her sweet hubby. "But if you're not out of here in ten seconds, I am going to put you to work hauling paint cans and carpet samples."

He held his hands up in surrender. "I'm gone."

He kissed her again, just a glancing peck, and headed out the door.

"Lunch!" she called after him.

He muttered a reply, but before she could chase him down to see if that mutter mattered, Sam waddled through the door connecting the old baby nursery and the new toddler room.

The boy had his tongue stuck between his teeth and his hands wrapped around the wire handle of a bucket filled with murky water.

"Oh, Sam! Don't bring that in here!" Hannah rushed to the child's aid. Or, as it turned out, to his downfall.

No, to the bucket's downfall.

Literally.

Down.

Down.

Down.

And *splat!*

Sam squeaked.

The empty blue plastic bucket bounced once, sloshing out the last bits of gray-brown liquid. Then it rolled quietly into the open doorway and stopped.

Sam didn't make another sound. No scream. No angry outcry. Just a timid little squeak. Then he stood there. Frozen. His shoulders hunched. His eyes huge.

He's terrified, Hannah thought. Terrified of what will happen to him because he made a mistake.

Without hesitation Hannah stepped across the ever-widening puddle of wash water soaking into the dingy orange carpet.

"My fault. I startled you." She gave him a quick hug, nothing too sloppy or sentimental, then flung into full-fledged distraction mode. "Did you get all the pudding out of the horsey's ears?"

There was a sentence that, before she became a mom, she had never dreamed she'd have any use for.

"I got some of it cleaned off." Sam sniffled. His lip trembled, but as soon as he saw her lunge for a roll of bargain-brand paper towels, he held out his hands to take some and dropped to his knees beside her to start sopping up the spot. "The saddle part was easy. And the rocker. But I can't get it all out of the nose or the ears."

"Hmm. I really had hoped we could use that thing." Their small church had gone through some upheaval in the past few years. They didn't really need much space or many toys for the young children. But with a new minister and a renewed commitment from the congregation, they had begun to grow. Hannah had hoped to stay one step ahead of that growth by planning ahead for the time when they could fill both rooms with kids and the things kids need. "But if we can't get every last bit of it cleaned up…"

He stood up and used the toe of his shoe to mash an enormous wad of paper towels into the sodden—and not particularly fresh-smelling—carpet. "Maybe if we took it to the car wash?"

"You going to ride it through, little buddy?" She dabbed at the edges of wet stain.

"No, but maybe we could strap it to the top of the mini-van. You know, on the luggage rack?"

"I am so onto you, pal." She sat back on her heels and laughed.

"Huh?"

"It wasn't enough that I humiliated myself in front of Stilton's mom with the nachos and the baby juice. Or came off looking like a slob in front of the DIY sisters when they stopped to find me doing my best Pippi Longstocking in pink fuzzy slippers on skunk-stink day. *You* want me to do something that the whole town can get a big chuckle out of." She poked him in the ribs, then spread her hands out as if to better visualize the whole scene. "Me and my minivan with an old, beat-up rocking horse strapped to the roof, riding through town like a one-woman parade!"

He covered his mouth and laughed.

She couldn't recall ever having felt so worried, so tired, so anxious and so happy all in the expanse of a few minutes. Well, not since the last time Tessa had put her through it.

Children.

How had she ever lived without them?

"I didn't think how it would look." Sam spun off some more towels. "It just seemed like it would *work*."

"You know what? It probably would." Hannah gathered the dirty, dripping towels into one large lump. She scooped them up in both hands, got to her feet and headed off to deposit them in the bucket. "That's what I like about you, kid. You are a source of almost boundless imagination!"

His eyes lit up.

"Boundless imagination! Did you hear that, Jacqui? It's almost as if Hannah heard us coming!"

"Jacqui! Cydney!" Hannah gasped, or did she gulp? Whatever she did, it was involuntary. At the sight of the sisters standing inches away in the toddler room doorway, all conscious thought had fled her mind.

"Good. We caught you!" Jacqui stuck out her hand.

In one fluid movement—a bit too fluid, as it turned

out—Hannah thrust the mess of waterlogged paper directly into the woman's open palm.

"Oh, no! I am so sorry." Hannah pulled back, snatched up the bucket and dumped the foul mess into it. "Really. So, so sorry."

"Don't be." Jacqui laughed—though not nearly as much as Cydney did.

"That's right." Cydney pushed past her sister into the room. She turned on her glittery tennis shoe and waved one hand in the air. "We don't mind getting dirty. We've come to help."

More like come to witness another of her disasters, Hannah thought glumly. Not that they had intended that, but more and more it seemed the obvious conclusion to anything Hannah did that involved interacting with normal human beings.

Hannah stepped into the hallway hoping the sisters would follow her lead.

Not only did they not follow, Cydney sat down at the table and began shuffling through Hannah's parcel of mail, humming as she did.

Distraction. That's what was in order.

It had worked with Sam. Why not the DIY-Namic Duo?

She gripped the handle of the bucket and retreated another step.

Thunk.

Her heel clomped against one of the paint cans she had yet to finish hauling to the church basement.

Suddenly she knew just what task she could use to get

them out of her hair—and, more importantly, out of her nursery.

"Terrific! So fabulous for you both to offer your time, but we're actually all done for the day here." She clunked the bucket back down and shook the last bit of damp from her hands. "Tidied up as much as we can for now and… Say, maybe there *is* something you two can do to help me out."

Jacqui tipped her chin up and shook back her short, sassy blond hair. "Name it."

"Well, you see, when I got here this morning, I found this room being used for storage, but I knew we were going to need it if we wanted to expand our infant and toddler programs. So, with that in mind, I started clearing the way, grabbing some paint cans and carpet samples and—"

"No!" Jacqui flashed her sister a stunned look, then turned to Hannah again, blinking slowly as she asked, "Really?"

"I…uh…" Hannah glanced at Sam, who looked a lot like he did the day he came in to find the dog had rubbed skunk spray all over their living room.

"Can you believe it?" Cydney shot upright so fast that her tot-size chair tipped over backward. She raised the rolled-up edition of the *Wileyville Guardian News*, like Lady Liberty lifting high her torch, and marveled, "I never dreamed I'd see the day."

"The day when someone would ask you…" Hannah motioned toward the pile of junk waiting for relocation.

"Ask us." Cydney pressed the paper to her chest. "*Us,* sister."

"I heard it." Jacqui held up her hand, always the one to remain calm and take charge. "But let's not go all flighty and ridiculous about it." She fixed her megawatt smile on Hannah. "We should have seen it coming, really. How could this lovely lady *not* have come to us to meet this exciting challenge?"

Hannah jerked her thumb over her shoulder toward the cans. "I wouldn't exactly call it a challenge."

"Well, what else could you call it—redecorating the baby and toddler rooms?"

"Re…re…" Hannah swallowed and forced herself to say it aloud. "Redecorating? You two? My nursery rooms?"

"Don't think of them as your nursery rooms anymore, Hannah."

"No?"

"Think of them as our canvas." Jacqui flung her arms out. Out.

What a lovely, compelling, unattainable word. It was all Hannah wanted right now—to get *out* of here so she could try to figure out what she'd just gotten herself *into.*

Think, Hannah, think.

"I, uh, I can't talk about this just now. Payt's at home fixing lunch for Sam and Tessa and me. Well…not for Tessa, but…we really can't stay."

Hannah swept through the room and into the nursery like a miniature tornado. Snagging Sam and directing him with a well-placed hand on his back, she gathered the diaper bag and her drowsy daughter up in one swoop, then turned to make her goodbyes.

She'd started the day with a single goal. To do the job she'd volunteered to do and to do it perfectly. And she had.

Except for the spill.

And the paint cans left in the hallway.

And the fact that she had just unleashed the DIY sisters on what she had thought would be her own quietly controlled territory.

Other than that, however, the day couldn't possible have been more perfect.

"Hannah Bartlett, why didn't you tell us?"

She jerked her head up to see Jacqui and Cydney poring over an open page of her hometown newspaper.

Oh, dear. What had Daddy gotten up to now? Somehow she'd thought that by living in another state she might escape the embarrassment of her father's lively antics.

Tessa squirmed against her shoulder.

Hannah adjusted the baby for comfort, and though she didn't want to, asked, "Tell you what?"

"About your writing."

"My…?" She edged forward.

"It's adorable *and* clever," Jacqui pronounced, like the arbiter of all things both precious and precocious. "Why didn't you tell anyone?"

"About what?"

"This!" Cydney shoved the open paper in her direction and smacked it with the back of her hand. "Your newspaper column about modern motherhood. Where did you ever come up with that title?"

"I…" She forced her eyes to focus on a strip of newsprint wedged between an update on who would be sending prized produce and livestock to the state fair next week and the list of new bus routes for the coming school year.

There it was. One of the worst photos ever taken of her in all its grainy newsprint glory just above the opening line Greetings From Nacho Mama's House.

Hannah didn't know whether to laugh or cry. So she just gave Sam a little nudge, snapped up the paper and her mail and headed for the door. "Excuse me, ladies, but we have to go home now."

"Are we going home to get lunch?" Sam asked.

"Yes, dear. We're going home to have a calm, pleasant, life-affirming lunch with Daddy. And as soon as we finish with that, I am going to kill your aunt Sadie."

5

Subject: What have YOU done?
To: ItsmeSadie
Journalism 101—always get the who, what, where, when and why. Since I am now—through no fault or initiative of my own—a newspaper journalist of sorts, let me ask you:

WHO do you think you are, publishing my private thoughts and stories about my life, written for personal amusement only, in the *Wileyville Guardian News*?

WHAT kind of thoughtless, pushy person does that to her own sister?

WHERE did you get the idea that I wouldn't mind seeing myself turned into a cartoonish buffoon in front of everyone in my own hometown?

WHEN did you plan to tell me that you'd done this?

WHY did you let them run a picture of me, eight months pregnant with my face puffed up like a water balloon, stuck right beside the headline County's Biggest Sow State Fair Bound?

I am never speaking to you again.

Call me.

"I'm a joke." Hannah slid against the wall to sit on the floor of her vacant front room.

"No." Payt settled down beside her.

"A laughingstock," she muttered.

"No. No." Payt wrapped his arm around her shoulders and pulled her close to his side. "People aren't laughing *at* you—they're laughing *with* you."

Hannah shot her well-meaning hubby a look that would boil stone. "Do you think saying that has ever made anyone feel better?"

"No, but it sure eases the guilt for the people doing the laughing." A smile lit his eyes.

She stretched out her legs and crossed them at the ankles. "Including you?"

"Yes."

She folded her arms and refused to look at him.

He jiggled her shoulders and rested his head to hers. "When it comes to this stuff you've written about your everyday adventures, yes, including me. I can't help it, Hannah, its funny. You're funny."

"Case closed. I *am* a joke."

"Okay let me rephrase that—your writing is funny. It's…it's…"

"Clever?" She borrowed Jacqui's description, because of all the things she could think to call her work, she could accept "clever." Not too pretentious. Not too humble.

"Yeah, clever." He kissed her temple. "You've got a lot of potential, kid."

Potential? The intended praise didn't help to unknot a single muscle. "Potential to make a great big whopping fool of myself."

He pressed his lips to her ear, pulled her closer still and murmured, "Or to succeed at the thing you've wanted to do since before I even met you, Hannah. This may finally give you the chance to be a writer."

A *writer.* Her breath caught high in her chest, straining her voice to the bare essence of a whisper. "I have always wanted to be a writer."

"I know." He pulled away just enough to turn her face to his.

When he gazed into her eyes, she saw love and sincerity mingled with something she rarely allowed herself to acknowledge—pride. Her husband practically glowed with pride over her abilities.

She looked away, unable to accept his endearing admiration. "I don't deserve to call myself a writer for this. What did I *do,* after all? Just typed out a few flippant notes to my family."

"What you did was what you always dreamed of doing, Hannah. You wrote something—and someone liked it."

"Wish you'd stop that."

"What?"

"Making me feel good about all this. Sadie tricked me. I don't want to feel good about any part of this."

"But you do."

She wriggled her back to the wall and scrunched her shoulders up like a child preparing for a tickle attack. And like that child, she couldn't hold back the slow grin that worked its way from deep inside her being to her tightly closed lips.

"I knew it." Payt laughed and hugged her again. "And I can't tell you how relieved I am."

"Relieved? Why?"

"Why? You'd ask that of the guy who has carried years' and years' worth of guilt over you quitting college and putting your personal goals aside just to help me pay for my education?"

"Just to help you become the man I knew you could be. The man you felt God had called you to be." She laid her hand alongside his cheek.

"Yeah, but you were the one who sacrificed for my goals."

"I didn't mind."

He kissed the inside of her palm.

A delicious shiver shot through her whole body. She relaxed, just a little, then held her hands up and out to indicate their surroundings and said, "Besides, look what all I've gotten in return."

"Yeah, a great, big, smelly, empty house." He grinned.

"Hey, this house may be smelly, but it's anything but empty." She swung her legs over his and laid her head on his shoulder.

"No, it's not empty. Far from it." He rubbed her back in a few brisk strokes, then tangled his fingers in her hair.

He kissed her cheek once and then again and then, before he kissed her one last time and murmured, "Nevertheless, I think there's still some room around here for *your* dreams, Hannah."

"Dreams? I have everything I ever dreamed of."

"Except—"

"No exceptions."

"What about writing?"

"I wouldn't know where to begin to pursue it, Payt."

"You've already begun. Contact the *Guardian News* and offer to write a column for them."

"A column? About what?"

"About the things you write to your sisters. About you, your life. About the kids. Maybe even now and then about your strong, intelligent, romance-novel hero of a husband."

"About *me?* About my *life?*" Didn't he understand? Exposing herself as the total, unmanageable mess of a person she was hardly made up the stuff of her dreams. In fact, it was her worst nightmare. "No. I don't think so."

"But you've got so much talent."

"Really?" Okay, she had an ego—even if it wasn't a very big one. "You think I have talent?"

"Don't you think you do?"

"I…I try not to think about myself very much."

"And if that statement there doesn't prove you have a natural flair for drama and fiction, then nothing does."

Her mouth fell open. She couldn't blink, much less speak. Then a primal, overwhelming urge filled her chest, until she thought it would explode. "I don't even know where to start with that remark, Bartlett. Do I tackle your implication that I *do* think about myself all the time, or your bald-faced audacity in calling me a liar by saying my opinion is a work of melodramatic fiction?"

"Bald-faced audacity." He chuckled. "See, you do have a way with words…Bartlett. And for the record, I never said *melodramatic* fiction or called you a liar. I just think your assertion is a bit…" He tilted his head, his voice trailing off.

"What? Tipsy?"

"No."

"Lopsided?"

"Ehhh, not exactly."

"Askew?"

"That one!"

"You're saying my thinking about your thinking about my thinking is *askew?* How could you say that?"

"I didn't say that. I'm not even one hundred percent sure what you said. But, hey, if the askew fits…"

"Do not try to kid your way out of this. I said I don't think about myself much, and you called that a pile of drama and fiction."

"Again, I have to defend myself. I didn't use the word *pile.* Though you are building it up much bigger than necessary."

She started to speak, stopped herself, started again and couldn't get a single intelligible syllable off her tongue.

"Shhh." He put his finger to her lips. "Let me help you out with this. I said you had a flair for the dramatic and for fiction. You've read and studied enough to know that pretty much all fiction boils down to a kind of fact cooked up into something more palatable."

"I don't know what worries me more—that you would compare my writing efforts to my cooking or that you are actually making sense to me." She pressed the heel of her hand to the center of her chest. Deep breath. In. Out. She made herself let go of the worst part of her instant physical reaction to Payt's seeming accusation. "Go on."

"Hannah, do you ever listen to yourself? Really listen?"

I try not to listen to myself too much. She discarded her initial response as quickly as it sprang into her head. Instead she chewed at her lower lip, raised one shoulder then let it drop in a halfhearted shrug.

"If you did, do you know what you'd hear? Aside from all the nice, sweet, smart and wonderful things you say—those aside, do you know what you'd hear?"

"I'm almost afraid to answer."

"Bingo." He touched the tip of his nose to show she'd gotten his point.

Then why did she feel so utterly confused? "Payt, I can't—"

"Bingo again! You are on a roll today!"

She prodded the gentle throb that had started in her temple. "I wish I *had* a roll—all this nonsense talk is making me hungry."

He laughed. "Listen. You said '*I'm* afraid.' You said '*I* can't.' And if I'd let you go on talking, pretty soon you'd have added, 'What will people think of *me*?' Sounds like someone who spends a lot of time and energy thinking about herself, doesn't it?"

The dull throbbing intensified. "Do I really come off so self-centered?"

"Not at all." He slid his hands to the taut muscles between her shoulder blades and began to massage. "Hannah, honey, it's not *that* you think about yourself. It's *how* you think about yourself. That's the root of your difficulty. It's what's stopping you from just taking this opportunity and running with it."

The warmth from his hands penetrated her work-weary muscles even as his message sank into her worry-weary heart. "I wish…"

"Don't waste your time wishing about it, Hannah. Think about it, sure. Pray about it, always. Then *do* something about it."

"Really?" Could it all be that simple? "You believe I can do it?"

"I believe you can do anything you set your mind to. You are a woman of extraordinary abilities, Hannah." He swept his hand up to push her hair aside and dropped a kiss on the back of her neck. "And you're a mighty fine writer, too."

She tipped her head back and exhaled slowly. "You are a wise but sometimes wicked man, Payt Bartlett."

"That's why you love me."

"That's not the only reason why I love you." She unwound herself from his embrace and scrambled to her feet. Standing over him, she offered her hand to help him up. "But, my oh my, does it sweeten the pot."

"So, you're going to forgive Sadie for submitting your letters to the paper." He didn't ask. He summed up. Done deal.

"Not in a million years."

He stood and brushed dog hair from his dark pants. "But she's your sister."

"And she, of all people, should know better than to hold me up to the whole town's scrutiny. All our lives, Daddy embarrassed us at every turn."

"He just acted like himself. You were the ones that *let* yourselves be embarrassed by it."

"Oh? How about when we were in grade school and he took on the whole Bouquet Belles system so that he could be a Garden Mother?"

"I think that's very sweet."

"And after our marriage ceremony, when he whipped a tin cup out of his jacket and asked everyone going through the receiving line for their spare change because the wedding had left him broke?"

"All in good fun."

"Fun? Maybe, but fun for *who?* Certainly not for me." Oops, she'd made it about her again. She cleared her throat and amended, "Certainly not for my *sisters*. Oh, and speaking of sisters, how about a couple years ago, when he purposely defied and disgraced Sadie by marching with the twirling tots in the Memorial Day Parade dressed as a cross between Colonel Sanders and a patriotic clown?"

"Okay, your dad is a loon. We all know that." He threw up his hands, but his grin never faltered. "You'd think that fact would make it all the easier for you to go with this, Hannah."

"Well, it doesn't." She twisted her hands together and walked to the sliding-glass door to look out over her meticulously trimmed lawn. "My oldest sister is over forty and runs around town dressed like a safari guide. She spends Sundays digging in her 'garden,' which is nothing but the median strip of the parking lot behind her plant shop."

"Leave April alone. She's doing all right."

"And…*my other sister*…" It was petty and childish not to say Sadie's name aloud. And Hannah didn't care. "The *other one* runs the cemetery—and likes it!"

"My nana Bartlett used to say, 'God loves a cheerful worker.'"

"Of course she did, because she was saying it to the dozens of servants who would rather have had a living wage than a pittance and some words to live by." Hannah hated dragging his family into this. Wasn't *hers* bad enough? She sighed hard, and clenched her teeth. "Anyway, my point is that it's all well and good for my sisters to have the town chuckling over *their* antics, but it's not for me."

"Why not?"

She lifted her hand and lamented, "Because I'm supposed to be the *normal* one."

"Yeah, so? Where's the fun in that?"

"Fun? I don't want to have fun."

Wait. *Had she really said that?* Everybody wanted to have fun.

And if, when they had their fun, they spread that fun around a little, what was so wrong with that? That was her daddy talking, of course. Easy for him to say. Despite his shortcomings, Moonie Shelnutt never had reason to doubt that he was loved and wanted.

Hannah shook her head. "No. No, I can't allow it. When Sadie calls, I will tell her just how I feel and warn her that I won't write so much as an instant message to her until I have her guarantee that she will never share another of my personal anecdotes with anyone."

"Anecdotes?"

"It's a word," she snapped.

"I know." He came up behind her and nuzzled the back of her ear. "A *writer's* word."

Writer. Her? The thought sent a warm shimmer through her entire body. Hannah Bartlett, wife, mother, *writer.*

R-r-r-r-ring. The phone yanked her back to reality.

Payt gave her an innocent nudge. "You better get that."

"Me?" She bristled. "Why not you?"

"Because I need to go check on the kids, and mostly because it's *your* future calling." He dropped a kiss on her temple, then turned to go. "Don't be afraid to answer it."

Her future? Her future didn't frighten her one bit. It was her past that always seemed to trip her up. How could Payt have lived with her so many years and still not know that?

"Hey! You play nice with your sister!" Payt's voice carried from the hallway through the empty living room.

R-r-r-r-ring.

Hannah took a step toward the children's rooms, away from the phone. "Is Sam playing too rough with Tessa?"

"Nope. I was talking to you, Hannah!"

"Very funny." She spun around, and before she had the chance to chicken out, grabbed the phone.

"Don't bite my head off." Sadie spoke first. "Just take a moment and remember your verse."

"'Peace. Be strong,'" she and Sadie repeated it together.

When Hannah, Sadie and April were little, their father had chosen a Bible verse for each of them. He probably had intended them as inspirations, but when a kid grows up having the sound-bite version of that verse thrown at them in every circumstance, the inspiration aspect starts to fade.

Hannah's verse was from Daniel, which she supposed fit—a lot of days her life did resemble time in the lion's den.

"'Peace. Be strong,'" Hannah repeated. "Too bad I'm not strong enough to reach through these wires and snatch you by the scruff of the neck so I could shake some sense into you."

"Me? What did I do?" Sadie's tone left no doubt—she knew exactly what she had done.

"What did you do? Only took my private thoughts and personal anecdotes…" *A writer's word.* Payt's gentle prodding came back to her. "You took my letters and held them up for public ridicule."

"Ridicule? Hannah, do you know what people around here have to say about your work?"

Her pulse fluttered. For a moment she considered begging her sister not to tell her. She'd spent her entire life cultivating an image of quiet sophistication, of good taste, of grace, of—

She caught a glimpse of her reflection in the side of the toaster. Her pale blue jeans bagged where the pudding-muddied water had soaked into the knees. Her hair stuck out every which way from Payt's running his hands through it. And the oversize bright green shirt meant to show off the skin tone she worked daily to keep perfect had baby spit-up on the shoulder. Grace. Sophistication.

Hannah laughed, more like a whimper really than a laugh, but still she served up a mincing smile as she asked her sister, "What do people around there say when they read about my life, Sadie? Do they say, 'Poor Hannah, tell her we're all praying for her swift return to sanity'?"

"Hardly."

"You mean they aren't praying for me?" Obviously they had never seen her after a day working in the nursery. She squared her shoulders. "That isn't very nice. You'd think someone would at least—"

"Hannah, stop talking about yourself and listen to me. *I* want to talk about you."

"Okay." It wasn't the kind of thing she could argue with, could she?

"Here's what people tell me when they read your work—Hannah is so bright, so talented. We always knew she'd end up doing something creative."

"Really?"

"Really. The day after they print one of your pieces, I have to put up with it all day long—Hannah, Hannah, Hannah."

"Wow! Wait a minute, after they print *one* of my pieces? How many of my e-mails have you sent in to the paper already?"

Sadie didn't miss a beat in her rant, much less bother to respond to Hannah's question. "And my favorite compliment—'Of you three girls, that Hannah has the best sense of humor.'"

"No way. No one says that about me."

"Yes. Absolutely yes. April and I are totally insulted, by the way. So much so, we talked about starting up one of those clown ministries to show everyone *we* can make people laugh, too."

"But, Sadie, I don't want people to laugh at me."

"Hannah, they aren't laughing *at* you, they're laughing…"

"Don't you dare finish that sentence."

"Peace, Hannah. I called to make peace, remember?"

"And just how do you propose to do that, after what you've done?"

"How about if I tell you the paper wants you as a regular contributor?"

"Doing what?"

"Your column, dope. 'Nacho Mama's House.'"

Hannah leaned against the wall and stared into her stark, disused kitchen. "Did you have to call it that?"

"It's cute."

Hannah groaned.

"Anyway, the paper can't pay much, but they *will* pay. Plus the editor says he will personally try to make sure your work gets seen by other sources, so you might pick up some freelance jobs."

"Freelance?"

"Jobs, Hannah. Writing. It's what you always wanted."

"Isn't that some kind of kooky curse? For people to actually get the things they think they want?"

"The only thing kooky is you, if you don't try this. Come on, Hannah, you have to try. If you don't, you may regret it the rest of your life."

"Sadie, do you sell plots in that cemetery of yours?"

"Um, no, why?"

"Because you're just very good at it, that's all."

"At selling?"

"Yeah, and at helping people dig their own graves."

"What does that mean, Hannah?"

"It means…" She squeezed her eyes shut and silently echoed the admonition from Daniel again. "Peace. Be strong." "It means tell them where to send the check. I'm going to write the column."

6

Subject: Opinion, please
To: ItsmeSadie, WeednReap
Keep in mind this is a rough draft. Sadie be kind. April, be honest.

Things really are cooking at Nacho Mama's house!

Really! My son's soccer team won their first game this week! Not that they won the first game they ever played, but after weeks of playing they finally won one! Ha-ha!

To celebrate, I wanted to do something special, and since I don't own a platter big enough to allow me to spell out Congratulations in nachos, I decided to bake a cake. A fellow soccer mom is on her way over to pick it up this morning to take to practice today. Guess I'd better get stirring!

Ha-ha. Sorry to couch my column in a bad pun, but speaking of couches, our furniture should arrive this afternoon—thus my inability to take afore-mentioned cake to practice. Also my aunt Phiz—that's my father's sister, Phyllis Amaryllis Shelnutt Shaffer Wentz—sent word a few days ago to expect a surprise today. Something from China, I suspect. I only hope it's not food, because it might get crushed in shipping. That's the way the cookie crumbles. You know, China? Cookies? Chinese fortune cookies?

Well, if you haven't guessed it by now, I might as well come right out and tell you. I have no business writing a column on the misadventures of modern motherhood. I am a phony. I'm not funny and I can't write and most of all I can't write funny.

Please, be wise. Do yourself a favor—do us both a favor—and toss this paper into the recycle bin with this column unread.

What do you think of your great idea to send my work to the paper now?

Sam dragged a beanbag chair across the living room, plunked it down by Hannah, then dropped onto it like so much deadweight.

The purple faux-leather, two-for-the-price-of-one accessory sighed, then crunched softly as he settled in. They'd let him pick out the pair of so-called chairs as a last resort to give them something to sit on and add a touch of hominess to their barren living room.

"Did you say hominess or home*liness*?" Payt had asked when they lugged the things in the house.

Sam wiggle-walked his chair closer to hers, stirring up enough static electricity to make a few of his hairs stand straight up.

She started to caution him about taking better care of the furniture, but one look at the green—according to Sam: "The exact color of lime Jell-O when you stick a flashlight in it!"—blob beneath her and she gave up.

Sam kicked his feet against the chair.

Hannah turned another page in the Bible that lay open in her lap. She knew he was bored. He'd told her so eleven times already, and it wasn't even 9:00 a.m. yet. The kid just wanted some attention, but between her writer's block and her I-can't-get-anything-right blues, she just didn't have the energy to entertain the boy right now.

Finally Sam leaned in to peer over her shoulder. When his chin touched the skin on her bare arm…

Pop!

"Ow." She rubbed the spot where the tiny electric charge had gotten her, then bent to give the boy's face a quick going-over. "You okay?"

"I'm bored."

"I know. But are you okay?"

"Yeah."

"Good." She went back her Bible.

"And bored."

She held her breath and tried to concentrate.

He leaned in more until his brown head obscured more than half of the book. "What'cha doing?"

"Looking up a new Bible verse that I think might work as my new encouragement."

He looked up at her, his nose crinkled. "Encouragement?"

"Motto?" That didn't really sum it up properly, either.

He shook his head.

"Okay, you know how Grandpa Moonie sometimes says, 'Peace. Be strong' to me?"

He nodded.

"Well, that's from the Bible. And my dad used it to…"

To make me feel like I could never measure up because no matter how hard I tried I never felt at peace and I sure never felt strong?

Unless anxiety-leading-to-inaction counted as a kind of peace, and hardheaded was the same as strong. Hannah lifted her gaze heavenward. "I just want to pick out a verse that fits me better."

"How will you know when you find it?"

"I don't know, hon." She sighed and closed the Bible slowly so that she could savor the smell of the leather and the rustle of the thin paper. Just holding the book gave her some measure of comfort, and she drew on it. "Truth be told, I'm probably just looking for a procrastination."

"Is that like a proverb? Where is it?" He slipped the book from her lap and opened the pages.

"What?"

"The Book of Procrastinations." The crisp pages fluttered as he flipped through, his eyes intent on the headers. "Is that in the Old Testament or the New Testament?"

"The Book of Procrastinations?" Hannah smiled. "Neither Old nor New Testament, sweetheart. Procrastination means putting things off. I suppose you might find those in the Book of Hannah."

"Show me."

"Oh, um, Sam, honey, I was making a joke."

"You mean Hannah isn't in the Bible?"

She blinked. "Actually, she is, but not as a book. Hannah was…"

"Show me."

Since Sam's arrival, Payt and Hannah had wondered how best to address what Sam's case worker had called "the nagging faith issue."

Being passed from home to home had exposed Sam to smatterings of beliefs and nonbeliefs. More often than not, the other members of Payt's family had tiptoed around the subject altogether, trying to placate the ever-changing moods of Sam's heartbroken father.

Now Hannah was awed to have Sam climb up beside her, hold open the Bible and say so simply, "Show me."

A lump rose in her throat. This was it. The awesome responsibility of helping a child find the way. It humbled her—and challenged her. On a gut level she wanted to push him toward the Gospels, to make sure he heard and understood the gift of salvation through God's only Son. But that was not what he'd asked. He wanted to see the book that told of Hannah and her great love for God and for her own son.

"Where is Hannah in the Bible?" He prodded again. "I can't find the name in the table of contents."

"You won't find it there. Hannah is mentioned in the Book of Samuel."

"Samuel? That's like my name, Sam."

"Yes, it is. Hannah was the mother of Samuel."

"She was?" His eyes got big. He held the book to her. "Show me."

"Okay, give me a minute. I have to admit I'm a bit rusty with where to find a lot of things in the Old Testament."

Sam jiggled his shoes while he waited.

Hannah hurried, conscious of the possibility of more static buildup and another shock. "Here. Here in First Samuel, the very first story is about Hannah and how she thought she couldn't have children."

"Is that like you?"

"Well, yes, actually, there were times I thought I'd never be a mom." Then she looked down at him. "But I had faith, and now I have two wonderful children."

He didn't say a word to that, but concern colored his expression.

She read the story of Hannah's prayer for a child and of Eli the priest hearing Hannah's grief and telling her to "go in peace."

"Like you again," Sam pointed out.

"Uh-huh." Hannah shifted in the beanbag and read on about Hannah having a son, concluding with 1 Samuel

1:20. "'…and gave birth to a son. She named him Samuel, saying, "Because I asked the Lord for him."'"

"That's not like you." This time the child spoke so softly she hardly heard him.

But his words imprinted on her heart.

Not so hard to do on a heart already tender from years of holding on to the very same pain—the fear of being unwanted. But Sam was *not* unwanted. And certainly not unloved.

"I love you, Sam," she murmured, pulling him into a hug. "It's true I didn't ask God to send you to me. But I did ask Him to give me a family—and here you are."

"Me and Tessa," he said.

Ooooh, how she knew that tone. The double-edged emotions of sharing a parent's love. Did she have to tackle the issue of sibling rivalry right now?

Sam provided her answer. He squirmed out of her arms, grumbling something about not getting all girly on him.

The moment had passed.

Sam leapt up and pointed to the Bible. "Did this help you with your procrastination yet?"

"Yes, it helped me procrastinate quite a bit." She shut the Bible and set it on the cardboard box they were using for an end table. "But in a good way, at least."

"Do you know what you're going to write about now?"

"Nope. Maybe I just need something interesting to happen around here to get my creative juices flowing." She stood up and rubbed her hands together like some mad plotter. "And it had better happen soon, before Tessa wakes up from her morning nap."

Tessa was a world-class nap taker. Hannah's sister Sadie told her to think of it as a blessing, but then Sadie didn't have to plan her day around a baby who was four hours awake for every one hour asleep during the day. Then reverse that in the night. The whole thing had Hannah near the brink of exhaustion. Which wouldn't be a big deal if she didn't keep taking on new projects that pushed her over the edge.

Which reminded her—

"I didn't finish frosting the cake yet. Mrs. Faison will be here in less than—"

Ding-dong.

"A minute?" she finished. She checked her clock. Almost an hour ahead of the time she'd said she'd drop by. Maybe the world's most perfect mom did have a flaw after all—*she showed up too early at places.*

Okay, as flaws went, it didn't rank up there with things like cussing, barroom brawling and wearing white after Labor Day. But it did show a chink in the other woman's armor and eased Hannah's apprehensions a tad as she said, "You let Mrs. Faison in, Sam, and I'll straighten up in here."

Sam took off for the front door.

Hannah glanced around the room with nothing in it but beanbags, a box and a Bible. Just to make herself feel like she'd done as she'd promised, she fluffed the bags, then stood back and eyed the effect with much satisfaction. "There. All done."

Sam put his hand on the doorknob and looked back at her.

She held up a finger to ask him to hold off unleashing Supermom into her home for one moment and made a mad dash for the kitchen.

"Now!" She gave the go-ahead even as she wriggled into her chef's apron, grabbed a cake spatula and pulled from the middle shelf of the fridge the tub of icing she'd mixed up earlier.

She heard the door creak as Sam eased it open.

Hannah took a deep breath and smiled. She'd heard that people could tell if you were smiling when you talked even if they couldn't see you. So Hannah smiled real big and said, "Come on in. You're just in time to lick the bowl!"

"That's just dandy, lady," a gruff male voice boomed through the wide-open spaces of her home. "Mind if we unload your living room suite first?"

The furniture? The deliverymen weren't scheduled to arrive until late this afternoon.

She tucked the tub of frosting in the crook of her arm and jabbed the spatula into it even as she rounded the corner from the kitchen to the front room. "You aren't supposed to deliver that until later."

"Sorry, lady, but our first two drop-offs weren't home. If it's a problem for you, we can put you on the end of the list and get back to you after we do the rest of our load—and the two we missed already. Might be late."

"No!" She jerked her hand up, forgetting about the spatula in it, and sent a blob of icing flying across the room. Without so much as looking in the direction of the glob of white dripping on the fireplace mantel, she gave a cheery wave of the kitchen tool to show her extreme composure. "I mean, no problem. Bring everything on in."

"Fine. Where do you want it?"

She looked around them. "I was thinking maybe in this big empty room here."

"Yeah?" He scrunched up his face as if he'd just taken a bite out of a lemon. "Here?"

"Um, yeah." She held her arm out to drive home the point. "Here."

"Okay, it's your house, lady. Not my place to judge." He shrugged, made a mark on the crumpled paper on his clipboard and headed out the door, hollering, "Bring it on inside."

"What was that about?" she asked Sam.

Sam cocked his head and held up his hands.

"Some people. Huh?" She didn't really know what she meant by that, but the moment seemed to need something more before she could sigh an "Oh, well" and get things rolling again. "Why don't you take Squirrelly outside so she won't be underfoot or try to run out the front door? And while you're out there, bring that tub of spackling compound Payt has in his work shed."

"The powdery stuff?"

"No. He saved some already-mixed-up compound in a clear plastic container with a blue lid—like we use to store leftovers and things around the kitchen."

"What are you going to do?"

"I've got to get this cake iced."

"With spackling stuff?"

"No. That's just in case the movers ding the walls—that way I can fill in any nicks or gouges before Stilton's mom gets here."

His look asked what he'd never voice: *What is it with you and Stilton's mom?*

She felt compelled to offer an explanation even though he hadn't actually said anything. "You only get one chance to make a first impression."

"Mrs. Faison has been here before."

"Yes, but that time came off less like an impression and more an indentation." She grimaced.

"Huh?"

She pointed toward the work shed. "Go."

In a whirlwind of bored-little-boy energy set loose, Sam grabbed the dog, hit the door and headed outside.

Hannah plunked the tub of frosting down on the counter and laid the spatula aside.

How did it go? Plop, then swirl the top, then the sides? Or sides first, top last?

"Wait." She held her hands up, suddenly recalling the class she had taken in cake decorating. "I'm forgetting something here."

She examined the rectangular cake sitting on a foil-covered piece of heavy cardboard.

"Let's see. Top. Sides. Frosting. Spatula." She ticked off the bits and pieces of the process she knew she had under control. "What else?"

The back door slammed shut. The pounding of Sam's shoes thundered through the whole house.

"Oh, crumbs!"

The boy pulled up short just six inches shy of hitting the side of the kitchen counter at full force. Tub of spackling compound in both hands, he looked up at her, breathing hard from his run. "Wow!"

"What?"

"I never heard you cuss before."

"I never… Oh, crumbs!" Hannah laughed. "No, honey, I just remembered I have to brush the crumbs off the cake before I ice it."

"Why?"

"So the crumbs won't get in the frosting."

"Doesn't it all get mixed-up together when you eat it?"

"Well, yes, but…" She made a motion in the air, trying to demonstrate the smooth surface she hoped to achieve. "Not important. Let's just say, sweeping of the crumbs makes me happy."

"You know that's really weird, though, don't you?"

She tipped her chin and held out her hand. "Hand me my spatula, good sir."

"Where is it?"

"I left it right…hmm, no." She spun around and checked in the sink.

"Can't you use old trusty?"

Could she? For an instant it was tempting…but only for an instant.

"'Fraid not."

He frowned at the rejection of his idea.

She placed her hand on his back. "But you can get old trusty out and test the spackling stuff to make sure it hasn't hardened. How about that?"

He flexed his arms to show his impressive muscles and announced, "Spackle-tester man."

"Go for it."

"Where would I be if I were a spatula?" She shuffled through the things scattered on the countertop, peeking under the edge of the cardboard cake carrier, lifting up a crushed paper towel. No luck. "Wait, I had it with the frosting tub in the living room."

Sam hoisted up the tub of frosting.

"Yup. There is it."

He set her tub down again and placed his carefully a few inches away.

"Now to dust for crumbs and get this show on the road." Hannah reached for the frosting.

Tessa's piercing cry made her jerk, which almost knocked the tub to the floor.

Sam caught it in time and pushed it back in place.

"Thanks. I'll go get the baby and be right back." She dashed through to living room with a glance out the open front door to see how far the deliverymen had gotten.

Beep…beep…beep. The truck backed slowly into the semicircular drive.

She sighed. At this rate there'd never be time to get the furniture situated, the walls retouched and the cake frosted before Lauren Faison showed up!

Hannah made the trek from front room to nursery in record time. A quick diaper change and a fresh T-shirt and Tessa could sit in her high chair and be a party to the goings-on from there.

"Hey, lady, what goes where in here?"

"Sam!" She called him to the nursery, and when he appeared in the doorway, she managed to call to him over her shoulder, "I'm up to my wrists in…"

He pinched his nose. "I know!"

"Can you tell the men to wait a minute?"

"I can tell them where to put everything, Hannah. I watched you and Payt walk around last night saying where to put stuff."

"Okay. Fine. It's not like I can stand and direct them anyway. And if I don't like where they set things, I can always move them." A year ago she'd have never imagined the skill with which she would be able to clean up a baby's bottom and simultaneously give a young boy instructions. "Let me go over this for you—big couch and little couch on either side of the fireplace, oak armoire on the opposite wall, coffee table in the middle. Anything else just set out of the way and I'll position it myself. Got that?"

He used his hands to show her the layout. "Big, little, oak, table."

"Great. I'll be in just as soon as—"

R-r-r-ring.

"Just as soon as the world stops spinning," she muttered. She stamped down the tab on her daughter's fresh diaper and picked up the child, drool-stained shirt and all, and headed for the kitchen.

R-r-r-r-ring.

Hannah eased Tessa into her high chair and turned just as Sam nabbed the phone from its stand. "Hello?"

"Whoever it is, tell them I can't take the call right now." In two steps she had globbed liquid soap onto her hands and thrust them under the faucet in the kitchen sink.

"Sorry, Mrs. Faison, she can't—"

She lunged for the phone, marveling that it didn't slip through her soapy fingers and go sailing through the air. "I can't believe it's you, Lauren."

She couldn't. She *really* couldn't.

"Yes, well, hate to impose, but Stilton's Tae Kwon Do lesson at our church fell through at the last minute."

And you want me to teach him how to break boards with various body parts? She had the presence of mind not to say the first thing that popped into her mind, though the image of beating her head against a two-by-four lingered even as she said, "That's too bad. What can *I* do for you?"

"Since we were already out running errands, I hoped you wouldn't mind if we stopped by a bit sooner than we planned?"

She *was* an early bird. But she called first. Of course she called first—otherwise it would be a kind of a fault, and this woman didn't have those.

"Fine, Lauren. I'm frosting the cake ri-i-i-ght—" she leaned over, dipped the spatula into the tub and slopped a dollop of frosting onto the cake "—now."

"See you in a sec!"

"A what? A sack?" Hannah stuck her finger in her ear. The movers had begun shifting furniture about, clunking and grunting and shoving things along the carpeted floor.

"Well, Tessa, honey, I hope she won't find me in a sack. Though if I thought I could find one big enough to hide in, I might try it." She waved the spatula, then started to work. "I shouldn't have let this frosting sit with the lid off so long. It's gotten dried-up and a little stiff."

More thumping, bumping and grumbling came from the next room.

She scraped the frosting from the edge of the blade, releasing the sweet scent of sugar and vanilla into the air. "Hey, Sam."

He peeked around the corner.

"How's it looking?"

"I can't tell. Everything's in plastic, but the big couch looks kinda small."

"Really?" She plunked the spatula down and stretched to peer around the corner at the plastic-covered lump in her living room. "Must be the love seat."

"Is that what it's called?"

"Yup. You can pull the plastic off if you want—I have to make this frosting work."

She heard the plastic ripping. Sam let out a whoop.

"At least someone is having a good time, huh, Tessa?" She stabbed the spatula in the tub and tackled the cake once again, but this time the thick white icing went on smooth and gorgeous. "It's working!"

She didn't dare stop now, not even when a loud *whump* shook the walls.

"What was that, Sam?"

"It's big and wooden—must be that arm ware."

"Armoire. It's—it's not important. Are they putting it in the right place?"

"Yes."

She took a deep breath and smiled down at the suddenly flawless waves of frosting on top of her soccer celebration cake. "At least something is going right today."

"Hello? Hannah? It's Lauren."

"Come on in. I'm in the kitchen."

"I see you've got your furniture."

"Today's the day for early arrivals. We didn't expect it until this afternoon. Pardon the chaos, by the way!"

"Don't give it another thought. Everyone's had some days when their house looked like—"

"Wow!"

Wow? Hannah mouthed Stilton's reaction. The furniture must look better than she remembered. She couldn't wait any longer; she wanted to see. If it wowed an eight-year-old, it must be…

"Retro chic?" Lauren skimmed her fingertips over the high-gloss finish of a full-fledged wet bar. Right there in her living room where her Mission-style armoire should have rested. "Is that what they call this, Hannah?"

"No! No, no, no, no! They call this a mistake. This is *not* our furniture!"

Hannah made a quick tally of the things deposited in her home. A leopard-print futon—the thing she'd thought was her love seat. A giant orange ottoman, on wheels, no less. A bar, with a glass back and rack to hang glasses overhead. And a pair of stools with dice and drinks on the cushions!

"This is not my home. This is somebody's rec room!"

Lauren touched her, shoulder to shoulder, and murmured, "Somebody with very…interesting taste."

Hannah looked at the open doorway. "Where are those delivery guys?"

Sam pointed. "Inside the truck."

"Maybe I should just get the cake and get out of your way so you can sort this out."

"Oh, yes, good." The sooner Lauren left, the sooner Hannah could fall apart. She motioned for the woman to follow her into the kitchen.

"I didn't have time to decorate it, but I bought some of those premade sugar decorations as a backup, so you can take those with you and put them on as soon as the icing sets a little more."

Lauren swiped her finger along the edge where some frosting stuck to the foil. "Um, Hannah, if this frosting sets anymore, it will be ready for wallpapering, not sprinkling with candy soccer balls."

"Oh, no." She couldn't have. Could she? She took a quick sniff of the flawless covering. "Oh, no!"

"What is it?"

"I had the frosting and some spackling compound for repairing the walls in the same kind of container."

"You frosted the kids' cake with spackling compound?"

"Not at first." She didn't know what made her feel worse—that she'd pulled another dumb stunt in front of Lauren or that her frosting hadn't been as smooth or as moist as a home-improvement product.

"You're having a rotten day, aren't you?" Lauren laughed, but not too much. Then put her arm around Hannah and added, "Don't worry. I'll take care of the snack."

"Let me guess. It will be something homemade?"

"Probably. If you don't think the kids will mind."

She opened her mouth to say something, though she had no idea how she could both convey her frustration over the ease with which Lauren handled everything and still sound grateful. Before she could compose a single comment, a commotion started in the living room.

A commotion. The spot-on perfect term for a seventy-something fireball with chopsticks protruding from her red topknot, wearing a pink dress and work boots.

"Surprise!"

"Aunt Phiz!" Hannah leaned back against the counter for support. "You said you were *sending* something."

"Yes!" She wrapped Hannah in her arms and gave her a kiss on the cheek. "I make it a policy to always send the best, so I sent…myself! Ta-da!"

Sam laughed.

"This must be Sam!" She swooped down to envelop the boy in her expansive arms. Then, looking up at Stilton, said, "And this must be…?"

"A friend." Hannah patted the boy on the back. "You really did pick a dilly of a time to pop in all the way from China, Aunt Phiz."

"Oh, my! Did I throw a monkey wrench into the works?"

Sam's eyes went all starry and bright. "Did you bring a monkey?"

"No, she did not bring a monkey." Hannah raised her gaze from the boy to her aunt. "Please, please, tell me you didn't bring a monkey."

Phyllis Amaryllis Shelnutt Shaffer Wentz burst into an uproarious gale of laughter.

Lauren joined in, politely covering her mouth with her manicured hand, but laughing all the same.

The boys began to leap about shouting, "Monkey! Monkey!"

Before Hannah could calm them, a bald man with sweat dripping down his thick neck crossed the threshold, his hands behind him gripping something huge. "Okay, lady," he asked. "Where do you want the Ping-Pong table?"

Aunt Phiz pulled herself together enough to pinch Hannah by the arm and shake her head. "You poor little thing. I guess I showed up at a very bad time."

"Actually?" Hannah looked around her at the laughter and the letdowns and couldn't help but think about her wish for something more exciting to write about. "You may have come at a moment of divine inspiration."

"How's that?" Lauren cocked her head.

"Let me rephrase that." Hannah folded her arms and made a mental note of every last detail of the bedlam surrounding her. "Can I use your real names in my column?"

7

Subject: Nacho Mama's House column
To: Features@Wileyvillenews.com
Big news!

We have a new addition to our family! No, not another child but rather someone with the faith of a child, the joy of a child…and the overblown, highly honed buttinsky instincts of a full-grown Shelnutt in her prime.

My aunt Phiz has come to help me out.

Before you get the idea I am typing about her behind her back, let me assure you that my aunt is completely aware that showing up for a two-week visit and inviting yourself to move in is the kind of thing that will get a person talked about. Aunt Phiz loves to be talked about. Almost as much as she loves meddling in the lives of her brother, his three daughters and their assorted spouses and children. So she won't mind one bit when I tell you that she came all the way from China to Loveland, Ohio, for the express purpose of making my life simpler.

Then why do I have this nagging feeling that my life is about to get a lot more complicated?

NOTE TO SELF: FINISH COLUMN BEFORE SENDING.

"As to any special dietary needs?" Phiz paused to clear her throat.

Presented with the first gap in the morning's meandering monologue, Hannah dove in. "Not to worry, Aunt Phiz. Cincinnati has a little bit of everything. Whatever you need, we can find it here."

"Me? Oh, don't you concern yourself about me, dear." The stout old gal patted her rounded belly and stretched out her bird-thin legs. An egg perched on stilts, Daddy had once described her figure. "I have the stomach of a goat."

"Lucky you. Sadie is like that. That girl can eat anything. She's the one who taught Sam that concoction of chocolate milk over cereal topped with strawberries."

Hannah cuddled into her plump new couch. The salesperson had promised her that the cheery checkered upholstery would withstand the assaults of two kids, a dog and whatever else they threw at it. She whisked the back of her hand over a berry-shaped chocolate stain and sighed. Obviously that man had never been to Hannah's house and seen what her family was capable of throwing.

Still… She smiled over her coffee cup and tucked her legs up under her. "That's right, you and Sadie and Sam, our family's very own three billy goats gruff, with stomachs to match. April has eyes like a hawk, and Daddy—"

"Your daddy is ornery as a skunk."

"I was going for crazy as a loon, but skunk works, too." Hannah laughed. "Meanwhile, me? I was blessed with hips like an elephant."

"Pfffttt." Aunt Phiz sputtered her distaste and scrunched up her deeply lined lips. "You have a darling figure."

"Yeah, darling if elephants are darling. Which I guess they can be, but mostly to other elephants."

"Stop that this instant." Aunt Phiz's delicate antique teacup, which she had hauled hither and yon around the world over the past two decades, clinked down into its saucer.

Hannah curled her heavy coffee mug, a freebie from a pharmaceutical rep calling on Payt's office, close to her chest. "Stop what?"

"Do you not know? Don't you even listen to yourself?"

"Why do people keep asking me that? Of course I hear myself. My voice comes right out of my mouth, conveniently located just inches away from my ears. I can't help hearing myself."

"Hearing and listening." She held both her index fingers up to demonstrate her point. She touched them together then whipped them apart, her jewelry jangling. "Not necessarily the same thing."

Hannah braced her bare foot against the edge of the new coffee table and pressed her lips together.

"And furthermore, your voice may come out of your mouth, young lady, but your words come from someplace else. Sometimes it's your mind. Sometimes it's your heart. Sometimes it's even your stomach." She patted her rounded belly and laughed. "Feed me chocolate now, and no one gets hurt."

Hannah's lips twitched, then relaxed into a hint of a smile.

"But in truth, what you say says more about you than simply the sounds you make. And, Hannah, what I hear you saying about yourself worries me."

"I just meant I'm not happy with my hips. That's all." *But was it?*

Hannah was no dummy. When two of the people she loved most in the world told her to her face that she needed to listen to herself more carefully, she had to take notice. But honestly, she didn't see how it would change a thing, especially about her hips.

She looked around at the new furniture that had taken six hours, three movers, eight phone calls and one near hissy fit to get installed in her living room. They'd been in Loveland such a short time, and while she loved the sweet little town, she had begun to wonder if she would ever settle in here. Every day some new thing confronted her that she felt ill equipped to handle. Even a simple dis-cussion with her aunt had gone so off-kilter that she suddenly felt the need to defend her interior life, her sense of humor, her very cellulite!

All she wanted was one day where she didn't have to endure a lecture on her shortcomings. Or face an uphill battle or downhill slide into humiliation brought on by her shortcomings. Or…or go through a day where she would be called upon to demonstrate her shortcomings.

Apparently, today was not that day.

She smoothed her hands down the legs of her pink Capri pants but the bumps and ripples and imperfections she saw there were not in the fabric. "Can we just drop the whole hearing and listening analogy for now and suffice it to say that Tessa is almost seven months old and I still haven't lost all the weight I gained."

"Fine. Yes. Fine. Let's not quibble." Phiz raised her age-spotted hand, setting her stack of silver bracelets clattering as she gestured in staccato movements with each word she spoke. "That brings us back to my question, though."

It took a full three seconds for Hannah to realize that her aunt expected an answer. "What question?"

"Dietary needs?"

"You want to know if I'm on a diet?" She folded her arms over tummy.

"Or have allergies or have any special restrictions, preferences or dislikes. Not just you, but the whole family. If I am going to be cooking for you I need to know."

"Cooking?" She unfolded her arms and dropped her feet to the floor with a thud.

It boggled the mind to imagine what exotic dishes Aunt Phiz might concoct. And how her family might react to them. What if they actually liked Aunt Phiz's Roasted Rack of Yak or Cream of Octopus Soup? Hannah couldn't even flip a decent flapjack, much less start off each morning serving up crêpes flamingo flambé. Hannah didn't even know where to get a flamingo in Ohio!

"That's so sweet of you to offer, Aunt Phiz, but I think we should stick with my brand of simple but nourishing style of cooking for the family."

"I've seen your handiwork." Even partially obscured by soft, crinkly skin, the older woman's eyes still sparkled.

Hannah raised her head. "I manage."

"And your family? They like these cakes with spackling for frosting?"

"No. They like…" They *liked* eating out. In fact they vastly preferred it to Hannah's effort in the kitchen. "Look, Aunt Phiz, I know I'm not the world's best cook but that doesn't mean I don't want to learn, that I don't want to get better at it."

The senior tented her plump fingers over her chest and leaned forward. "I'm listening."

"I've waited so long for the chance to do just that, to take care of my very own family." Hannah gazed into her secondhand mug and swirled the dregs of her coffee around. "Surely you understand?"

Her aunt lifted her teacup and sipped her aromatic, anise-flavored tea. Her eyes searched Hannah's face for a moment before she set the cup back on its saucer with a decisive click. "Not only do I understand, but I think I know precisely how to help you realize that very thing."

"Help?" she asked weakly, when deep down inside she wanted to fling open a window and scream it. *Help! Help!*

"Never fear, Hannah, my darling. Aunt Phiz is here, and she is going to teach you to become a first-class gourmet cook!"

Cooking lessons. She guessed she could squeeze those in, somewhere between mothering, writing, running the nursery and…

Aunt Phiz pushed up from the oversize floral wing-back. Everything from her hair to her boot laces swung into the action as she waddled off to the kitchen, her precious teacup in hand. "Get the kids ready. We are going shopping!"

Who knew?

All these years everyone teased her for being a lousy cook when they should have teased her for being a lousy shopper!

Okay, it wasn't quite that simple, but standing in her own kitchen now piled high with a shiny new collection of pots, pans and gadgets filled Hannah with a soaring sense of unlimited potential.

She could study the recipes in her new cookbook.

She could listen and learn and do her aunt Phiz proud.

She could make…meat loaf!

"Turkey meat loaf." Aunt Phiz waved her hand over the ingredients strewn along the cluttered countertop.

"Turkey? You sure about this?"

"Considered a healthier alternative by some."

"Some as in someone whose name rhymes with Shyllis Shamaryllis?"

"Humor me." She slapped the meat, wrapped in bright white paper, into Hannah's palm. "And get cooking. We're burning daylight."

"Okay, but do me a favor. Don't use the words *cooking* and *burning* in the same breath around here."

"You'll do fine. Just follow my instructions."

8

Subject: Nacho Mama's House column
To: Features@Wileyvillenews.com
Last week the hardest questions I had to answer were:

"How do you know when the meat loaf is done?"

"Do you want extra cheese on that pizza, lady?"

And "Why, when Aunt Phiz said she came here to help us, do we have to wait on her?"

The answers:

"You can always tell when my meat loaf is done by the sound of the kitchen smoke alarm going off."

"You're asking Nacho Mama if she wants extra cheese?"

And—

"Because, son, your foster mommy is a wimp."

Oh, for those simpler times when the only thing anyone expected from me concerned the Aunt Phiz factor and the proper way to dispose of flaming turkey meat loaf. I'm afraid those days are long gone.

The days of the DIY-Namic Duo have begun.

Sort of.

Let's just say that they've begun to begin.

We've moved the cribs and rockers and toys into the fellowship hall. It's a short-term thing—meaning I've come to terms with having my meager authority usurped, but if the sisters don't move things along I'm going to get a little short with them.

Especially if they don't stop asking me questions like "Runners or puzzle mats?" I said runners. I have no idea what they were talking about, but as a long-time wearer of panty hose I have some experience with runners. On the other hand, while I don't know this Matt fellow, I have no desire to sic the sisters onto the poor man with the express purpose of puzzling him.

Kidding. Honestly. Don't write to explain that runners are strips of carpet and puzzle mat is spongy safety flooring. I do know the difference. If you have to write to offer your help, please, please, tell me how to encourage two highly enthusiastic women that actions speak louder than words. Even their words.

Their lots and lots of words.

Especially when those words are aimed directly at

me, asking me the kinds of questions that I am totally unprepared to answer.

NOTE TO SELF: FINISH COLUMN BEFORE SENDING

"Canary or Kumquat? Canary?" Jacqui pulled one four-by-four-inch square slowly back, then whipped a second one up and demanded, "Or Kumquat?"

Hannah blinked at the two paint-sample cards held inches from her nose. She chewed her lower lip, trying not to let the pressure steer her toward the wrong answer. She felt the way she did at the optometrist's office when he said, "Better like this? Or better like this?"

But at the eye doctor she only ran the risk of getting the wrong prescription and spending the next year trying to look at the world through glasses that she didn't really need. Flub this choice and who knew how many infants might spend their Sunday mornings in a nursery that could fail, as Jacqui put it, "to stimulate their minds and generate feelings of creativity and security."

Yikes!

At least she only had one DIY sister to deal with on this. Cydney had staked her claim in the toddler room and at this very moment stood sketching a mural of Noah's Ark on one wall of the adjacent room. At least Hannah thought the rough pencil lines would eventually represent Noah's Ark.

Though she had to admit she got that idea more from the singing going on in the next room than from anything Hannah saw on the wall.

"C'mon, Sam." Cydney's voice carried through the partially opened door between the two rooms. Loud as she spoke, it could have carried through walls. "One more time, but this round give it all you've got. Throw in a little *oomph!*"

Sam obliged, belting out at the top of his lungs, "'The Lord said to Noah, There's going to be a floody, floody…'"

"Hannah!" Jacqui snapped her fingers.

The song faded to a background buzz.

"Canary or Kumquat?"

Hannah studied Jacqui's face for some hint of what she expected. Finding nothing but intense anticipation, Hannah finally sighed and blurted out, "Um, Canary."

"Canary?" Her voice cracked.

"Did I say Canary?" Hannah glanced at both squares again. Squinting, she pushed her fingers through the fringes of red hair that had escaped her once neat little ponytail. "Kumquat. Definitely Kumquat."

"You don't think it's too…?" Jacqui crinkled up her nose, exposing the deep lines in an otherwise flawless face.

Hannah involuntarily crinkled her own nose. She squinted, trying to determine the problem with the deeper tone of the two colors. But she couldn't see it. "Oh, no. Absolutely not."

Jacqui held at arm's length the color sample Hannah had chosen. "What about Lemongrass?"

"What about it?"

"Do you like it?"

"As what?" She'd had nightmares like this. Where people spoke to her and she had no concept of what they meant or of what they wanted her to say.

"A color." Jacqui darted to the paint-spattered tarp bundled against the wall, seized another small card and flipped it around to show Hannah. "How do you like it as a color?"

Hannah shook her head. "I don't know."

Jacqui exhaled in a short, sharp blast.

No one could describe either of the sisters as tall or, upon first glance, physically commanding. But when one of them wanted to get her point across, she had the presence of a giantess. And the gestures to match.

"Lemongrass. It's a color. A very lovely color. I showed it to you last week." She bent at the knees, arched her back and waved her hand over her shoulder to indicate the past.

"Last—" Hannah waved, too, though weakly and lacking any real direction, much less conviction "—week?"

"We thought it veered too much to the green." On the word *we,* she made a circular motion, as though some unseen committee had come to this conclusion.

Hannah copied the movement Jacqui had made with both hands but used only one finger in a very half-hearted whirl that ended with her finger pointed to herself. "*We* did?"

"Too institutional." Jacqui bobbed her head as if nodding for the whole invisible team. "We opted for something that trended toward gold."

Hannah struggled to recall such a discussion.

Flooring? She remembered that.

Window treatments? Yes. She'd even made a bad pun about needing treatments to get over the trauma of looking at all those window treatments.

But trending toward gold?

She tipped her head to one side and winced. "Gold?"

"Not Goldenrod or American Heritage Mustard, not that deep of a hue. More of a hint of gold. Kissed by gold, as it were."

"Kissed?" Hannah rubbed her forehead.

"That's what *you* wanted. A vibrant, warmer tone."

"I did?"

"Yes, *you* did. *You* wanted a warmer color. So I brought warmer colors." She raised the sample squares. "Now *you* tell me you can't decide?"

Got it. Hannah exhaled. Message received. In Jacqui's eyes, Hannah clearly had created all the problems. And she knew just how to fix that. "Okay, I can decide right now."

"You can?"

"Yes."

"Wonderful. So which is it? Kumquat? Or Canary?"

Hannah shimmied her shoulders in triumph and smiled, ready to accept her accolades as she said decisively, "Lemongrass."

Jacqui threw up her hands.

The paint samples somersaulted through the air.

Kumquat, Canary and Lemongrass dotted the floor at her feet.

"What did I do?"

Jacqui shut her eyes. "Perhaps—"

Hannah licked her lips.

Jacqui cut herself off with a broad, slashing motion through the air between them.

Hannah cleared her throat.

"Hannah, I—" Jacqui pressed her lips together. She held her index finger over her mouth as if it took that measure of control to prevent a regrettable outburst on her part.

"What?"

"Excuse me a moment, would you please?" Jacqui spun on her heel to leave. Every last thing about her, from the soft click of the heels of her turquoise loafers to the swish of the dark curls at the back of her head, told of tightly reined-in fury.

But why? Clearly Jacqui had wanted the Lemongrass shade all along.

"I wanted to be accommodating," Hannah told Tessa as she scooped her up from the baby seat.

A door slammed down the hallway.

Hannah jumped.

It opened again with a whoosh of air.

Crisp, clipped footsteps came toward her, then stopped cold.

The singing halted midphrase. Just "'Rise and shine and give God—'"

Then nothing.

A quiet commotion next door followed, rapid-fire murmurings.

Hannah bristled. She clenched her jaw. "If I weren't the world's most accommodating person to work with, why would I even be here this afternoon? Much less have hauled you and Sam along? He only has another week until school starts—we should be out doing something fun."

Tessa gurgled and slapped her hand lightly on Hannah's cheek.

"Don't you start in on me, young lady." Hannah smiled and kissed the pudgy pink fingers. "At this point you and Sam are the only people in the whole world I know who without a doubt still think I am not a total disaster. And I'm not too sure about Sam."

"Not too sure about me about what?"

"Not too sure if you saw that steam coming out of Mrs. Lafferty's ears or not." She motioned to the side of her head and hissed to lighten the moment.

Sam tiptoed fully into the room, whispering, "She sure is mad."

"Sssssss." Hannah drew more invisible heat waves in the air shooting from her ear and laughed, but inside she felt anything but jovial. Tears stung the rims of her eyes. She chewed her lower lip to keep from sniffling.

"Why is Mrs. Lafferty so mad?"

"Because…" Hannah had gotten herself into this because she couldn't tell these sisters what she really thought. Did she dare share that unbecoming little tidbit with Sam? She gazed into his earnest, sympathetic eyes. "Oh, honey, I can't say for sure why someone else feels what they feel. Or even *if* they feel what I feel they feel."

"I feel dizzy." He put his hand to his head and wobbled his way down to sit on the floor.

Hannah laughed. "Okay, let me try again. What I think happened is that Mrs. Lafferty thought I was not putting enough thought into her project. So I thought I'd try to make her happy by telling her what I thought she thought I ought to think was the right choice."

He scratched the tip of his nose with the back of his hand. "You thought she thought you thought what?"

"It doesn't matter what I thought, Sam. The end result is that I tried to think of how to please someone else by telling them what I thought would make them happy so they would think better of me, and now I'm sunk."

She sighed, her shoulders slumping.

"Awww." Sam wiggle-walked on his knees over to put his arms around her legs. "Don't be sad."

"I'm sorry, Sam. I should never have dragged you and Tessa in here today to quibble over Kumquat, Canary or Lemongrass."

"Huh?"

"Paint colors," she explained, pointing to the squares lying on the floor.

"They all look yellow to me."

You want to see yellow? You should look at the streak down my back. Hannah withheld the comment. Sam didn't need to hear her insecurities spilled out for a laugh.

Listen to yourself. Payt and Aunt Phiz's words echoed in her mind.

And she had heeded them. She had listened, really listened.

She had spoken to herself and in the same instant caught it and paused. If it wasn't the kind of thing fit to say to Sam, why would she consider it suitable to say to herself, about herself?

Somewhere in that convoluted reasoning, the seed of change had just been planted.

She knew it even as she knew she had no idea how to nurture it. Only that she must nurture it. For her children's sake. For her own.

She would start doing that by stopping this nonsense with Jacqui. Now.

"What do you think, kids? Do you have an opinion about what color we should paint the toddler room?"

"You know they all look the same to me." He got to his feet, plucked up the pieces of paper and offered them to the baby. "But why are you asking Tessa?"

"Well, of the three of us, she'll spend the most time in here." Hannah swiped her thumb over her daughter's damp chin. "What do you say, sweetie? Shall we see which one you drool on the most and go with it?"

That process would make about as much sense to Hannah as Jacqui's did. Who cared if the room ended up with a greenish tint or a golden one?

The baby fisted her hands around two of the cards and let the third fall away.

It tumbled down and down and landed color side up.

"Bye bye, Lemongrass," Hannah muttered.

"She's picking!" Sam hopped from one foot to the next.

"Okay, this is it, Tessa. Kumquat or Canary?"

The child squealed.

"Kumquat? Or Canary?" Hannah leaned closer.

Tessa stuck both arms out straight, waved them about for a moment, then poked one balled-up card into her mouth.

"We have a winner!" Hannah pulled the card away from Tessa.

The baby protested with a kick and a screech.

"Now she's mad, too."

"She'll get over it."

Hannah kissed the baby's head, inhaling the sweet scent of her fine curls.

Tessa quieted—a little.

"She'll get over it, and so will Jacqui. Tessa didn't have any business hanging on to that paint card. Just like Jacqui doesn't have any business hanging a paint color over my head."

"Was Mrs. Lafferty mad enough to pour paint on your head?

"Maybe, but you know what?"

He shook his head.

"I am not going to let her do it. I wouldn't let her actually do it and I refuse to let her do it metaphorically."

"Metawhatically?"

"Vocabulary lessons later, son. Right now I have a job to do." Hannah tweaked Sam's nose. "Your mommy is *not* a wimp. She's an intelligent, capable person who can speak her own mind."

"What does that mean?" Sam blinked up at her.

"It means we're done here today. Let's go enjoy the last days of summer." She nudged her son to get him going.

He hurried on ahead.

Hannah took one last look at the slobbery sample she'd

slipped from Tessa's grasp, then wedged the corner of the card under the plastic light switch cover.

She flipped off the light in the toddler room, calling over her shoulder as she ushered her family out the door, "Canary!"

9

Subject: Nacho Mama's House column
To: Features@Wileyvillenews.com

Rat-tat-tat-tat-tat-tat. Rat-tat-tat-tat-tat-tat. Rat-tat-tat-ta-ta-ta-ta-tat ta-dum. Ta-dum.

That's right. If my life were to have a theme song right now it would have to be the one they play to accompany plate spinners, jugglers and acrobats.

Plates-a-spinning big-time around here—figuratively and literally. But I am getting better at juggling Payt's, Sam's, Tessa's and my own schedules. And like some out-of-control acrobat, I have my share of tumbles. Of course, I still think I'd look ghastly in tights!

The cooking lessons forge on. And by that I mean the results look like I produced them in a forge not a kitchen. Pork roast isn't supposed to have the color and consistency of pig iron, is it?

Aunt Phiz's palate is proving more exotic than our small-town tastes around here. I didn't do a bad job with the eggplant Parmesan but Payt wouldn't have any part of it. Not until I likened it to fried green tomatoes—then he couldn't get enough.

Oh, and while I'm on the subject—breading! Why didn't anyone tell me about this minor miracle years ago? Flour, egg, bread crumbs.

The great equalizers.

Unfortunately breading does not work its magic on soccer kids' snacks. Have tried to get away from the nachos in favor of more healthy choices. Yesterday Aunt Phiz whipped up a batch of oatmeal cookies. I spent the rest of the afternoon making faces on them with raisins for eyes, apple slices for mouths and shredded carrots for hair.

They ate the cookies.

I think they fed the apple slices to the dog.

The shredded carrots are ground into my carpet.

The raisins?

Found some between the couch cushions.

Some dropped down into the vase on the bookshelf.

And two stuffed inside the ears of Payt's bust of Dr. Albert Schweitzer.

It's hard to stay mad at the boys, though. They are really good kids, even if they are rotten soccer players. Sadly they haven't won another game yet. Am I a bad mother because I'm secretly a little bit relieved because this means I don't have to attempt another cake?

No cooking for me tonight, though. Aunt Phiz is watching the children and I am going on a real, live bona fide date—with my husband! He left a message on the phone for me to meet him at his office after hours so we could catch up together. Trés romantique, n'est-ce pas?

At last, one evening in my life I won't end up writing jokes about!

NOTE TO SELF: FINISH COLUMN BEFORE SENDING

"You asked me here to do what?" Hannah stood in the vacant waiting room looking at the top of her husband's lowered head through the opened frosted sliding-glass window.

He scrubbed his clean, blunt fingers through his shortly cropped hair, never lifting his gaze to her. "Start by emptying out the trash cans, then tackle the break room."

"Trash?" She tugged at the pearl necklace Payt had given to her when she'd given birth to Tessa. She'd only worn it one other time. Funny, she hadn't noticed it feeling so constricting then. "Tackle?"

"Dump the small wastebaskets into the big one on wheels by the back door. In the break room, tidy up. Clear away. Do whatever needs doing to the floors, that kind of thing." He tucked a pen with a drug company's name on it in the front pocket of his lab coat. "Oh, and bin liners in the supply closet."

"Bin liners in the supply closet to you, too," she muttered, shifting her weight.

Her feet already ached in her brand-new high-heeled sandals, the kind of shoes she'd worn all the time before becoming a mom. Their soles scuffed the floor as she moved toward the receptionist's desk. "Payt? Isn't there something more you want to say to me?"

"Hmm? Oh, yeah." Payt rummaged through the book where the staff recorded phone messages. "Turn out the lights when you leave a room. Don't want Dr. Briggs to show back up and find us wasting electricity."

"Dr. Briggs? Tell me you did not drag me down here to try to impress the phantom Dr. Briggs." He wouldn't. He couldn't.

"I'm on a ninety-day trial period. Clock's ticking."

He had!

And all for Dr. Raymond Briggs. The boss. Senior partner. The surrogate father figure in Payt's work life. Had to please the man. Had to do whatever it took just for the hope of an "atta boy" and a place at the proverbial grownups' table.

Where, if her husband didn't start thinking about the consequences of his choices, Payt might end up sitting alone. Not that Hannah had any room to criticize. Aside from taking on the column and choosing Canary for the toddler room, what had she done to break free of her own childhood patterns? How had she ever tried to rise above her own longing for approval?

Not much, she thought, standing in the office all dolled

up for a date and not daring to demand her husband at least discuss the situation with her.

That had to end.

This was Payt, after all.

If she couldn't assert herself even a little without risk here, she might as well give it up for good.

"In the first place, if you are here working after hours and asking your wife to work here, too, after hours—even though technically a person not getting a paycheck doesn't have 'hours'—then whatever electricity you use can hardly be called wasted." Hannah took a few steps toward the closed-in reception area.

"I know. You're right, but Dr. Briggs—"

"Is *not* coming back here tonight." She'd met the man who had taken Payt on as a junior partner a whopping total of two times. Even so, Hannah grasped the improbability of the fiftysomething, single-again-and-had-the-foreign-sports-car-to-prove-it man returning after hours for a "lights-out" check. "At this very moment Dr. Briggs is probably filling himself to the gills at the Maisonette or wherever it is men of his ilk stuff themselves."

Payt's dark brows slanted in over the most innocently perplexed eyes in the world. "What's your point?"

"At least tell me that while you're putting in overtime here, Dr. Briggs has taken on call for the night."

Payt shook his head, almost smiling as he said, "I was going to be working anyway."

Hannah groaned and started to rub her eyes. Her fingertips touched her mascara-coated lashes. The first time she'd worn more than a smidge of makeup in months. She didn't want to smear it all over the place. So she cupped her hands over her cheeks and dropped her gaze to the floor.

"I'm not saying to turn the lights off while you're in the room, Hannah. Just have the courtesy to hit the switch on your way out when you're done."

"If I were going to hit anything on my way out, Bartlett, it wouldn't be the switch." She folded her arms and waited.

"Thanks, sweetie. I'll be in my office catching up on paperwork." He slid the glass partition closed between them.

"Catching up. This is what you meant by catching up?" All she saw was a blur where her husband had stood moments ago.

He had cut her off. In every way possible. Visually. Verbally. Audibly. Emotionally.

As she stood there with her mouth open and heart exposed, her initial responses of denial, determination and even the first wash of anger evaporated. And shame flooded in to take their place.

"I shouldn't. I don't deserve a new outfit," she had told Aunt Phiz, who had encouraged her to pull out all the stops. "This money should go for something the kids need. Besides, someone who hasn't lost all the weight from her baby shouldn't indulge in clothes. What if it makes me too comfy in my new shape?"

"It will make Payt happy to see you looking so pretty," her aunt had countered.

And Hannah had bought it. The line of reasoning and the pretty dress.

Pride had made her do it, and she knew better. What did she have to be proud of?

As for making Payt happy? Obviously she could have accomplished that in coveralls and a hair net, or a sweat suit or…any outfit that said she had come to get some work done. Hannah took a deep breath.

Hmm. No "doctory" smell of rubbing alcohol, the astringent odor that had made her pulse race as a child. Not even the odd clash of freshly baked goodies brought in by clients and sterile biohazard-approved disinfectant spray that permeated the clinic in Wileyville. This place smelled…*empty*.

And she didn't like it.

She kicked off her sandals and set them carefully by the door. She had run the gamut of emotions. What else remained but acceptance?

Or action.

Why not? She'd stood up to Jacqui Lafferty. And Jacqui Lafferty was a lot more intimidating than Payton Bartlett, boy-faced pediatrician.

"Payt, honey." She pushed through the door and made a beeline for the tiny back office that Payt had inherited from the other two young pediatricians Dr. Briggs had driven off over the past five years. "What are you doing here?"

He stood right beside the door collecting pieces of paper from a plastic "in" box. "You wouldn't believe how many forms I have to deal with in a day."

Don't start with me about not knowing what your spouse deals with in a day. You are the absolute king of that.

Early in her marriage she had learned not to let every sharp or sarcastic thought she had pop out of her mouth. She'd learned that from watching—and listening—to her sister Sadie, who never seemed to let a smart-mouthed remark go unuttered.

That wasn't the way to win friends or mend marriages, Hannah thought. So she entwined her fingers in front of her. She pulled back her shoulders. She drew in the warm, lingering scent of the peanut butter and jelly sandwich she'd made Sam as part of the chaos of getting out of the house, and the perfume she'd spritzed on her neck just before coming into the silent waiting room. And she said, "I appreciate how hard you work, Payt. But—"

"Some of these cases, Hannah—" he raised his gaze but did not meet hers "—they'd break your heart."

"Oh." How could she have acted like no one else figured in this scenario? Payt had patients. Sick little children depended on him to ease their suffering.

"And if I don't check all the right boxes and fill out the right forms, the hassles with insurance can shoot these poor parents' stress levels through the roof."

"Never thought of that." And she'd been ready to read him the riot act for not paying enough attention to her.

Her. With the two beautiful healthy children, the big-hearted husband and the meddling aunt come from halfway around the world to help with them all.

For someone who liked to think she never thought of herself, she sure did think a lot of herself.

"Give me forty minutes, and if you're not done, I'll pitch in and we'll knock off the cleaning," he muttered.

Cleaning. She hated to seem ungrateful, especially on the heels of such a humbling moment but… "You know, when you called today you never said a word about cleaning. I, uh, I actually thought you invited me to dinner."

"Dinner! What a great idea. Let's grab some burgers or a pizza on the way home." He bounced a kiss off her cheek and turned away to begin leafing through a stack of files on his huge, dark cherry desk.

"Payt!"

He worked a single page loose from the brass brackets in the file in his hand. "What?"

She held her arms out to her sides and shook her head.

With the paper wedged between his thumb and first knuckle, he swept his fingers back through his hair, leaving it as disheveled as his expression looked dumbfounded. "What?"

She let out a soft sigh and tried not to laugh at her adorable but clueless man. "Not what, honey. Why?"

"Why what?"

"Why have me come to your office to empty trash and clean the break room? Don't you have a service for that?"

"I asked Dr. Briggs the same thing, and turns out he, um, that is, *we*…don't." He waved the paper hard enough to make it crackle. "Gotta run make a copy of this."

And he slipped away.

Hit and run. Deliver the bad news, then disappear. The man hated confrontation. Always had. So on those rare occasions when he couldn't charm his way out of dealing with unpleasantness, he avoided it.

Unfortunately for her hubby, this tactic wasn't going to work. Not anymore. She *now* had experience with eight-year-olds.

"Payt?" she singsonged ever so sweetly, padding barefoot behind him down the hall.

"Yes?" He parroted her tone.

"Even if you don't have a cleaning service, you do have a staff."

"Hmm?" He slid the paper into the copier.

"You know, the people who make the mess in the first place. Shouldn't they clean up after themselves?"

He punched the copy button, and the machine whirred to life.

"Shouldn't they be doing the cleaning, instead of me? It's not that I mind a little hard work but…you do have a staff for that kind of thing. Right?"

He pulled out the copy and examined it a little too long before grabbing the original and brushing past her, saying, "We have a staff, Hannah, but they aren't here right now, and now is when the work needs to be done."

She clenched her teeth. Her cheeks burned. Not in anger but because she felt like such a dope.

Obviously he didn't want to tell her why he'd asked her in to do someone else's work. Or maybe he just didn't understand *why* she wanted him to tell her. Either way, it made her feel…disconnected. Dismissed. Just plain dissed.

He didn't mean it that way. She knew he didn't mean it. But…

"Payt, honey, can't you just tell me what's going on?"

His eyes searched her face.

For a second she thought he might just tell her to mind her own business. No, strike that. He'd tell her to mind him and his business and stop presuming she deserved an explanation.

He'd never done anything like that before.

She had no reason to believe that he ever would.

But in her anxious heart, in the depths of her imagination, in the fears and self-doubt that bubbled just below the surface of her practiced persona, she suddenly suspected he wanted to.

Then he heaved out a world-weary breath, shook his head and, wearing a sheepish grin, he leaned against the door frame. "I'm so embarrassed, Hannah. How could I have been such a fool?"

"Fool? You?" *Him? Not her?* The very suggestion set her pulse skipping. "Payt, what are you talking about?"

"Politics."

"Local or federal?"

"Office."

"Oh." She winced. She'd worked a lot of years in offices to pay the rent and put food on the table while Payt pursued his studies. "Office politics—the trickiest kind of all."

"You don't know the half of it." He crooked his finger. "Walk with me."

She put her hand on his back and kept pace with him step for step.

"Raymond's office." He moved swiftly past the closed door with the brass plaque proclaiming Dr. Briggs.

She wished she could have poked her head inside and learned a little more about this man who had her husband hopping whenever he said, "Jump." But Payt had moved on already.

"Dottie." He pointed into an office that made his look like a broom closet. "Office manager and bookkeeper. Been with Dr. Briggs through three pediatric partners, two wives and at least one total office meltdown."

"Oooh." Hannah peered in, noting the photos of grown children and presumably grandchildren gracing the bookcase. Then her eyes fell on a painting that as an old Kentucky girl she recognized as a prized thorough-bred. She smiled. "What do you call her? The war-horse?"

"She's earned the title." Payt laughed and strode on, swinging his arm out to point into the next room. "Kaye. Nurse Practitioner. If Dottie is our warhorse, then Kaye is the big dog."

Hannah sized up the cheery room lined with painted children's chairs, an overstuffed sofa and a zillion stuffed animals filling every nook and cranny. "Just guessing, but looks like the big dog's bark might be worse than her bite."

"Guess again." He raised his eyebrows, then snaked his arm around Hannah's shoulders to motivate her to get moving again.

"What's this?"

"Break room." He pointed with the papers in his hand. "Also serves as Meg's quasi-office on the days she's here."

"Meg?"

"Part-timer. Nurse. Comes in for shot clinics and… whatever."

"Whatever? Okay. So if Dottie's the warhorse and Kaye's the big dog, what's Meg?"

"Cash cow."

"Payt!"

"She knows that's her function here. And she's too young and too cute to be offended by it." He shrugged. "Her husband runs a clearinghouse of services for children in need—he sends us a ton of referrals."

"Okay, so far I can see why you're not ordering anyone here to empty trash. But what about the receptionist?"

"Heather?" He twisted his head to stare in the direction of the closed-off area in the waiting room and sighed. "The scapegoat."

"What are you running here, a pediatric office or a petting zoo?"

"Sometimes I wonder myself." He laughed a careworn laugh and shook his head. "It all boils down to Dr. Briggs decreeing that no one but Heather should have to clean up."

"Let me take it from there." She held her hand up. "When Heather does clean up, the other women blame her for everything they can't find, or find in the wrong place or just plain don't like around the office."

"The scapegoat." He nodded. "How'd you know?"

"Did you forget that I worked in doctors' offices for years?"

"I didn't forget. That's why I called you to pitch in and take the heat off Heather. It's hard enough trying to establish myself in a practice that has spit out two other doctors in the past five years. So I decided to play peacemaker."

Peacemaker at the office. But what about in the home? He'd taken into account every woman's reactions to the job at hand except Hannah's.

If he'd only asked her opinion on all this. If he'd only *asked* her anything instead of just telling her to meet him and getting her hopes up.

"You didn't mention a word of this when you called me today."

"Didn't I?" He scratched his jaw with the back of his hand, the stubble making a quiet scraping sound in the still hallway. "Hmm. Sorry about that."

"You didn't even tell me that you wanted me to come in to do housekeeping chores."

"Well, again, sorry." He leaned over and kissed her temple.

He lingered there a moment, probably dead tired on his feet.

She closed her eyes and savored his closeness just the same. She loved this man. She loved the way he stood just enough taller than her to make her feel secure but not overpowered. That at the end of the day he smelled of antibacterial soap and lollipops. That he felt warm and soft and rugged and strong all at once, and that she could feel all those things standing here next to him.

For all the things she loved about this man, she still wished…

"Sorry to call you in like this." He moved back, waved the papers and turned toward his office again. "But I knew you wouldn't mind."

"But…" she whispered as she watched her darling husband disappear into his cubbyhole of an office. She brushed her fingertips over her pearls and fought to keep her lip from quivering. "I *do* mind."

She did.

And she was well within her rights to mind.

She blinked at that realization. Her hand closed around the necklace and she waited for a lightning bolt to strike her for even thinking about her feelings and not just snapping to, glad for something more to do to show her husband how much he could rely on her.

No lightning.

No overwhelming wave of anxiety.

Just a sense of calm. Of resolution.

Sure, she'd clean the office up this time. But not again. If this ever happened again, she'd give her husband a piece of her mind. And she knew exactly what she'd say.

"You told me I don't listen to myself, and that's the root of my problems. Well, I've started listening to myself—a lot. And if I listen to myself too much, it might just be because no one else in my life seems ready to hear a single thing I have to say. And that has got to stop."

10

Subject: Nacho Mama's House column
To: Features@Wileyvillenews.com
Tessa speaks!

Oh, all right, she belched.

And hiccuped.

The combined effect did sound like a primitive attempt at communication. I have it on very high authority—Sam's—that what my darling baby daughter bellowed out was her first-ever opinion of the state of things at our house: "Yuck!"

I have a hard time arguing about it. It sounded just like that. "Yuck!"

And her expression backed it up.

And Sam, standing right beside her as he modeled new clothes for his great-aunt, concurred. "Yuck!"

You don't think the impending first day of school has colored Sam's judgment any, do you?

Sam has dreaded the start of school. I know this because he can't stop telling me all about it. And by "telling," I mean whining.

He whines while I do the shopping.

He whines while I bathe the baby.

He even whines while I try to talk to Payt about how much the boy is wearing me down with all his whining.

It would drive me crazy (crazier?) if not for the picture he makes.

There he stands, socks drooping, eyes darting, brow furrowed, hugging his soccer ball and setting forth his case. He wishes he didn't have to go to school. He wishes he could just go on having soccer practice and playing games with the guys. No amount of telling him that going to school would not mean an end to soccer satisfies him. By the way, I checked this whole end of soccer season matter out thoroughly. Not only is there no rest for the wicked, there is no back-to-school reprieve for Snack Mom. Kids' soccer, it seems, knows no season.

"We want you to want to go to school. You're going to like it" has become the steady refrain around here. Payt and I try to work it into every conversation.

Sam pouts.

Tessa belches and hiccups.

Her discontent I can handle with a dietary change.

Sam's? I'm afraid all the cooking lessons in the world won't help me make going to a new school palatable to an apprehensive little boy.

NOTE TO SELF: FINISH COLUMN BEFORE SENDING.

"Where did you go to school, Hannah?"

"In my sisters' wake," she muttered.

Payt laughed.

She shot a warning look across his profile.

He cleared his throat and adjusted his grip on the steering wheel.

"I don't get it," Sam said. He swung his foot, and the heel of his brand-new shoe landed on his blue backpack with a dull thud.

"Just making a joke." She shook her head, but that didn't quite jar loose the memories of her own school days.

"Why aren't you more studious like your sister April?"

"Why aren't you more social like your sister Sadie?"

Why aren't you less like you and more like…someone lovable? That's how the constant comparisons had echoed in her child mind.

"Hannah?" He poked the backpack again, and the lifeless lump of a thing slouched forward, bumping the back of Hannah's seat.

Startled back to the present, she gyrated her shoulder to keep her seat belt from choking her when she looked at Sam and asked, "What, hon?"

"Did you go to the same school the whole time?" He kept his gaze focused out the window, his hand on Tessa's car seat strapped in beside him.

"Well, technically I changed schools when I went to middle school and high school, but they were all Wiley-ville schools."

"That must have been great."

"Great?" Hannah followed Sam's hollow-eyed line of vision to watch the sun-brightened streets of Loveland go rolling slowly past. It was such a pretty part of town, old enough to be quaint, kept-up enough to be pricey. It reminded her of Wileyville, the way it appeared in chamber of commerce brochures, not the way it really looked. "I guess it was great, in a lot of ways."

"Payt? How about you?"

"Yeah. I went to the same school for a while. Then my dad sent me to military school."

"Military school?" The boy blinked. "Did you learn to be a soldier?"

"A good little soldier," Payt murmured under his breath.

Hannah touched her husband's wrist.

"Be a good little soldier" was what Payt's mother had told him when they loaded him on the bus that took him away from his home for the first of many times. It probably wasn't the first time he'd gotten the message that his parents' love was conditional, something earned, but it was the one that stuck with him.

"Yeah, they tried to teach me how to act and think and

carry myself like a soldier. Couldn't seem to get the knack of it."

"Then, after that, you went to the same school for a long time, right?"

Payt laughed, but only out of the corner of his mouth, as though he couldn't give his whole self over to the humor. "You know, sport, I never went to the same school for very long. Even after I stopped flunking out of school and failing at jobs I'd taken to learn a trade, I didn't get to stay in one place too long. College, then med school, then to a hospital for my internship. After that the clinic in Wileyville, and now here."

"Wow. You've started over even more than me! You must have got real good at it by now."

"No matter how many times you do it, starting over is always hard, kiddo." He squinted at the line of cars stopping at a red light in front of them. "But having people who believe in you makes it easier."

Hannah gave him a look that, if Sam had seen it, he'd have called all girly and gooey.

Her husband reached over, took her hand and brought it to his lips lightly.

"Good job," she mouthed.

He caressed her fingers before letting go and muttered back, "Thanks but it was pretty clichéd, don't you think?"

She snuck a look over her shoulder, then whispered, "Hey, when you're Sam's age, you haven't heard any of this stuff. Nothing's clichéd. Besides, it's true and it's the right message to give him."

Payt's simplified answer had seemed to mollify the boy for the time being.

They rolled up to the light as it turned red again.

"Is that clock right?" Payt reached over to tap on the face of the digital clock built into the dashboard, as if he could jar it loose and suddenly give them more time. "We should have allowed for traffic."

"No rush." Hannah stretched her legs.

"You said school started at eight."

"School starts at 8:35. I said we should try to get there around eight."

"Why?"

"To provide for unforeseen circumstances."

"Like roadwork." He frowned at the brief snarl of traffic ahead.

Hannah lowered her head and peeked around the side of her seat at the young boy fidgeting with his safety belt in the back of the van.

"Like life circumstances," she said softly.

Sam let go of the shoulder harness, and it slapped against his chest. He didn't flinch or even seem to notice, just sat there staring out the window.

"All these cars can't be headed to the same place we are. Why can't we make any headway?" Payt made it through the intersection only to come to a dead stop again.

A million hopes and fears did their own version of gridlock in Hannah's being.

"No rush," she whispered again.

Payt gave her arm a squeeze, then raised his head to speak to Sam in the rearview mirror. "You're going to do fantastic in this new school, pal."

"Okay, I'll try. I just…" The child folded his arms over his belly and bent forward.

Payt shot Hannah a laughing look.

Tessa threw a colorful cloth teething toy at Sam.

He batted it away and hunched his shoulders. "I just hope I'm well enough to make it through the day."

"Hmm. Well, maybe we should cruise on past the school and head straight for Payt's office to get you checked out?"

Sam stayed all scrunched over for a moment, then slowly straightened. "That's okay. I kind of feel better now."

"Do you?" Hannah asked.

"Huh?"

"Feel better? *Really?*"

"No. Not *really.*"

"Want to tell us about it?" Hannah asked.

Sam shook his head.

They drove the last few blocks to the school in silence.

Payt pulled the van into the small parking lot and found a space.

This was it. Big moment.

First day of school.

Hannah held her breath.

She and Payt had toured the long-established nonde-nominational school twice before deciding on it for Sam. They had gone through new student orientation and met with the school administrators, Sam's teacher and her aide. They'd even seen the class hamster.

Sam had reacted to it all with resignation.

Hannah had wanted to give the child every reason to look forward to the experience, but Payt had asked her to hold some details back. He did not want them to build up Sam's expectations only to have them dashed by a last-minute change of plans.

That's what Payt had said, "change of plans." What he'd meant was that he feared Sam's father might have a change of heart and want the boy to go someplace else to live and attend school.

Hannah pushed the possibility aside and had gone about trying to prepare Sam to take the fourth grade by storm. All the coolest school supplies. Crisp, clean spanking-new uniform. She had done all she could to make sure Sam was ready.

But nothing she had done or could do would have gotten Hannah ready for this moment. All summer long it had been her and Sam and Tessa. Payt and Aunt Phiz and the soccer kids, too, but mostly the three of them. Together each and every day, learning from each other. Now Sam had to go off and learn from someone else.

"You know, all of a sudden *my* tummy doesn't feel so good." She laid her hand over her abdomen.

"C'mon, don't lose it now. Everything will be all right." Payt got out of the van.

The sliding back door rumbled as he pulled it open for Sam.

Tessa waved her fist in the air.

Sam watched the baby for a second, then bent to pick up her toy and handed it back to her.

"C'mon, kiddo," Payt urged.

The boy kicked his backpack one more time, then heaved it up onto his shoulder and hopped out onto the blacktopped parking lot.

Hannah got out and scanned the lot. Here and there families stood beside cars, adjusting uniforms, making little speeches. Moms dabbed their eyes. Dads cleared their throats.

Corny as it sounded, the whole thing eased Hannah's worries just a little. She'd done such a checkered job as Snack Mom, she'd hate to have failed at being school mom by being the only who didn't handle the first day's parting with absolute cool.

A gust of wind blew up from behind and tossed her red hair over her face. She started to slip her sunglasses on and poked herself in the eye.

Cool. Like that ever was an option for *her.*

Shading her watering eyes against the sting of the morning sun, she tossed her sunglasses into the van and slammed the door.

The instructions sent home for parents clearly stated they should not accompany the children inside the building. Volunteers stood waiting at the curb to shepherd the students to their rooms.

Hannah leaned one hip against the side of the van, stay-

ing near the open side door to monitor Tessa. "I should
have signed up as a room escort."

"Oh, yeah, you have time for that." Payt patted her
back. "Let it go, Hannah. Let *him* go. God's got this covered, you know."

She knew. But sometimes didn't God deserve a little help?

"Okay, pal. Here you go." Payt rested his large hand on
the boy's thin shoulder. "Any questions, concerns or true
confessions before you head off?"

Sam pulled on the neck of his uniform shirt.

A few feet away two little girls squealed at the sight of
one another and ran headlong into each other's arms.

Sam frowned at them and placed his open hand on the
van door. "Did you have friends in school, Payt?"

"Sure. I guess." He shrugged.

"Did you have friends, Hannah?"

"I had sisters—does that count?" She worked up a meager smile.

Sam nodded. He took one bold step away from them
then twisted around, his face pale. "What if…"

Hannah's heartbeat swelled in her chest. She swallowed
hard and bent at the knees to make better eye contact.
"What, honey?"

"What if I don't make any friends?"

Friends!

"Oh, no." She winced. In her anxiety, Hannah had forgotten to tell him the news about the school, the news
Payt had wanted her to hold back until they knew for sure
he'd attend.

"What if nobody likes me here?" Sam pressed on before she could get a word out. "What if I don't get asked to any birthday parties? At the last school I didn't get asked to any parties at all."

"Oh, Sam." She held her arms open to the boy.

For a second or two she thought he wouldn't come to her.

Then he inched closer.

And closer.

She held her breath.

He ducked his head. He rubbed his knuckles over his nose.

She didn't try to force things between them, just waited and watched.

His lips twitched.

He wasn't going to come to her.

Her jaw tightened. She didn't dare blink for fear she'd tear up.

"Sam," she whispered so softly, she doubted he even heard her. She brushed his back with her fingertips, then started to stand.

In a flash, the small boy rushed forward and flung himself at her, wrapping his arms around her so tightly that she almost fell over backward.

"Sam." She laughed against his coarse straight hair. "You don't ever have to worry about being alone again. You have me now."

"And me," Payt chimed in.

"And Payt." Hannah hugged the boy hard enough for the both of them.

"And Grandpa Moonie," Sam added as he stepped back, his eyes filled with hope.

"If you want to claim him."

"Hey!" Hannah lifted her index finger to warn Payt to behave.

Her hubby grinned. "Then yes-sir-ree, you got Grandpa Moonie one hundred and eighty percent."

"And Aunt Phiz." Sam tugged his backpack firmly into place.

"Sure. And don't forget Tessa." Hannah nodded toward the baby flailing her legs and arms about in the confines of her car seat.

Sam wrinkled up his nose. "Tessa's a baby."

"But she likes you. Haven't you seen the way her face lights up and her whole body wriggles when you come into the room?"

"Yeah?"

"Yeah." Payt jiggled the pack on Sam's back to shift the school supplies down so the thing didn't throw the kid off balance. "And don't forget, wherever you go, God goes with you."

"I heard Aunt Phiz say that God isn't allowed in schools anymore."

"Some people want that, but that's just because they don't understand that they can't tell God what to do or where to go. He's everywhere." Hannah fussed with the boy's collar. "You just have to pray. And before you tell me prayer isn't allowed in school, it *is* in this one."

Sam whooshed out a long breath. "Good."

"And that's not all." Hannah drew her shoulders up. "You know this school we picked out for you?"

"Uh-huh."

"You know why we picked it?"

Sam looked at the blond brick building with the bright red doors. "Because it's a Christian school?"

"Yes, that, and also because we got some personal recommendations about it."

Payt had worried about the expense of private education but Hannah had put her foot down. They had no idea how much time they would have with Sam. They owed it to the child to give him as much as they could for as long as they could. That meant an education that exposed him to the values they shared in a clean, safe environment. It also meant helping him to feel less isolated. To give him the gift of not just being loved but the blessing of being *liked*.

"You know who recommended this place to us?"

He shook his head.

"Stilton's mom." Yes, Hannah had turned to her exemplary counterpart for guidance. If anyone knew the best, it would be Lauren Faison. "Stilton goes to this school."

"Really?"

"Yup, and his mom says that a couple of the other boys on your team go here, too."

His mouth hung open for a second before he narrowed one eye and cocked his head. "Just 'cause they go there doesn't mean we'll be in the same class."

"Well, that's why *you* are headed to school, young man. *You* don't know everything. This school only has one class in each grade."

He looked at the school, then at Payt, then Hannah, then the school again. "So I'll be sure to have my friends in my class? For sure?"

"For sure."

"Yeah!" Sam gave a little jump, then pivoted and ran off as fast as his legs would carry him.

"Sam, aren't you going to give me a goodbye hug?" Hannah called out.

"I don't have time now. I want to go to school!" He never looked back, just charged on through the doors and down the hallway.

"Bye, Sam." Hannah sniffled. "I'll be here to pick you up at three."

Payt put his arm around her and nuzzled her cheek. "Now what's wrong? I thought you wanted him to want to go to school."

"I did. But I didn't want him to want it that much."

11

Subject: Nacho Mama's House column
To: Features@Wileyvillenews.com
Sam needn't have worried about not getting invited
to any birthday parties. Two invites have hit the mailbox already. Hit being the operative word! I'm shell-
shocked—or maybe that's sticker shock.

What happened to simple kid's parties? These
things look like Hollywood extravaganzas. I expect
paparazzi and armed security.

Okay, it's not that bad. But I can't help wondering
what will we do when it's our turn to host Sam's birthday? Renting out a water park and hiring a cement
mixer to flood the water slide with nacho cheese
springs to mind.

Better hit the warehouse club and start stocking up now!

At least we have a few months before we have to deal with all that. In the meantime other worries about Sam weigh on our hearts.

Dear readers, I try to keep things light and show you my world through love and laughter, but if I may break from that for a moment—

I'd like to ask those who are so inclined to remember Sam and his situation in your prayers. I know I've mentioned that Sam is our foster child and that we have no control over how long he stays with us. I'd have used a false name for him in the column but 1) Sadie submitted the first ones without my knowing it and 2) Y'all know who he is anyway. But to the kind ladies who asked for his full name to add in prayer, I hope you understand why I can't divulge that. Just say Sam. God will know who you mean!

We certainly appreciate the thought, though, as we have come to love this child as our very own. Whenever the topic of long-range plans arises, it is always with the unspoken thought in our hearts: What if Sam isn't still with us then? In his young life the child has lived in multiple homes and gone to more schools than most of us attend in a twelve-year educational career.

That's too much turmoil for anyone, much less a young, shy boy.

He needs stability. He needs continuity. He needs

to trust that there are people in this world on whom he can always depend.

We all do.

Please remember Sam in your prayers—we're counting on you.

NOTE TO SELF: FINISH COLUMN BEFORE SENDING.

"Can I count on you then?" Everybody needed somebody who could always be counted on. And today Hannah needed everybody she needed to count on to come through for her. Starting with her aunt. "Aunt Phiz?"

"Yes, dear, go right on talking. I'm listening. I've done this so many times, I can do it blindfolded."

"Blindfolded, huh?" She studied her aunt.

Wearing a blue-and-orange kimono, Phiz massaged her freckled fingers through a crop of brilliant red hair—a shade not normally found in nature, much less on a seventysomething-year-old woman.

Hannah plunked her elbow on the table and rested her chin on her hand, musing, "Beauty treatments done blindfolded. That explains so much, Aunt Phiz."

"Oh, you." She waved off the gentle teasing and padded barefoot through the kitchen clutching to her chest a grocery bag full of permanent wave curlers. "Run through your schedule for me again, dear."

"Mmm." She sat straight and shimmied her upper body then lifted her shoulders left then right, to try to release some of the tension that never seemed to entirely leave her body. When that didn't work, she sighed, poked a spoon-ful of mushy cereal into Tessa's mouth and said, "I have a morning meeting with the DIY sisters."

"The *D-A-F-F-Y* sisters if you ask me." Aunt Phiz fixed a towel around her neck with a big yellow plastic clip they usually used to keep potato chips fresh in an open bag. "Have they ever finished their takeover project?"

"It's called a *make*over, Aunt Phiz." She watched her baby for a reaction to the new taste sensation.

The baby's whole body tightened. She made a face.

Hannah braced herself. "And no, no progress to speak of yet. Every time we talk, they have one teeny more thing they want to add."

Tessa swallowed. Her eyes grew wide. She stuck her feet out, toes pointed, and poked her arms out straight to ask for more.

Hannah thought she must have given birth to the single most adorable baby on the planet.

She fed her daughter another spoonful. "They must be nearly done by now. Why else would they want to meet with me?"

"Maybe they want you to approve them wallpapering over the stained-glass windows in the sanctuary."

Tessa gobbled down the cereal and thumped both hands on her high-chair tray.

"Very funny. Your aunt Phiz should go into comedy full-time, don't you think, Tessa?"

"I'll do that when your mama goes into the travel business."

"Travel?"

"Why not? You've become a whiz at herding those little ones into new and more exotic places every Sunday, all the while smiling and asking sweetly when the cruise directors on the good ship Follypop think the decorating will be done."

"When you put it that way, it does sound like a takeover."

"Does it?" She hummed lightly while she dunked her tea bag in her favorite cup, one hand still holding the bulging bag of curlers.

"You know it does but…wait a minute! You sidetracked me. The subject was you sitting with Tessa, not the sisters walking all over me."

"Of course I'll sit with Tessa, dear."

"Terrific. I won't take more than two hours. Three if they don't want me there."

Aunt Phiz laughed and gave Hannah a quick hug in passing. "How could anyone not want my Hannah Banana? Just let me finish doing up my hair."

"Now?"

"Well, yes. Now. What did you think I was up to with all this?" She held the grocery bag aloft and shook it like a cheap maraca.

"Aunt Phiz, I almost never know what you're up to. Or when. Why do you have to do your hair now? Can't it wait until I get back?"

"Hair waits for no woman, my dear." She jumbled the frayed mass of red sticking every which way on her head.

"I'd love to oblige you, but the lady from across the street has kindly agreed to come over and help out."

"I thought you could do it blindfolded."

"Not the back anymore. Can't keep the old arms up like I used to." She yanked back the delicately decorated kimono sleeve to reveal a pale, aged arm. "Perhaps I should take up weight lifting?"

"Maybe you could start with lifting some of my load." She shouldn't have snapped, but with Sam in school and Tessa getting her eating and sleeping habits sorted out for the first time in weeks, Hannah had actually looked forward to getting out by herself. "It's not like I ask you to pitch in very often."

"I know, dear. And that's precisely why I'm unavailable to you so often."

"There's some logic swimming around in that murky pond of your reasoning. I just know it."

"Yep." Aunt Phiz tipped the bag up and sent a cascade of colorful plastic curlers clattering over the tabletop.

"You going to share it with me, or do I have to go fishing for it?"

"Always the first to take action." The older woman began sorting the curlers by color. "You never could wait for something to come to you—you had to go and get it."

"This is no mere pond of confusion. It's a whirlpool. Round and round." Hannah swirled her wrist, and rotated her head to illustrate her point. "You're trying to make me so dizzy I can't remember the favor I asked you. Is that your plan?"

"The only twirling round I plan includes these and this." She held a pink perm rod up to a strand of hair to demonstrate. "I planned to do this days ago. I had time to make these plans because despite my having come here to lighten your load around the house, you never ask me to do anything."

"Now. I asked you *now*."

"And when I offer to do anything, you refuse to let me."

"When?"

"When I asked you to let me get up with Tessa sometimes at night."

"She's my first baby. Her crying wakes me up anyway. Why should I put you out?"

"Fine. Then how about when I made those cookies for Sam's team and suddenly you're there sticking raisins and apples on them and taking over the whole project?"

"Just trying to live up to my title of Snack Mom." She held her hands up to frame her face.

Aunt Phiz *tsked*.

Hannah dropped her hands into her lap. "It's not like that worked out to make me look good. They ate your cookies and left my finishing touches…untouched."

"You wouldn't even let me clean up the raisins."

"My mistake. My responsibility."

"Mine, mine, mine. I think that might have been your first word."

"Doesn't anyone in my family have something nice to say about me?"

"Everyone in your family has wonderful things to say by you." She pursed her lips as she spoke, the same way they talked to Tessa when she pitched a fit over a dropped toy or fought off an onslaught of strained peas. "But none of that would mean a thing if we never spoke the truth to you, as well."

"Okay. Fine. Speak the truth, Aunt Phiz."

"You sure?"

"You flew from China to Loveland for my benefit. I'd be stupid not to take advantage of your input."

"*Stupid?* Pretty strong word to use about yourself."

"You going to lecture me about how I talk to myself, too?"

"Just taking note, dear." She took a sip of tea, waggled her head, made a silly face at Tessa, then focused on Hannah again. "And by the way, I flew here from India, not China."

"I knew that." She bumped the heel of her hand to her forehead. "You probably think I'm so wrapped up in myself that I didn't realize I kept saying that wrong."

"I don't think you're wrapped up in yourself, Hannah."

"Mine, mine, mine?"

"Your first word. Simple. Innocent, really. Your way of declaring your independence…and your insecurities. Your whole life, I've seen those forces at war within you."

At six years old, Hannah's sister Sadie had pushed her off the monkey bars and Hannah had had the wind knocked out of her. This felt a lot like that.

"But you know, sweet girl, insecurities and the driving desire for independence—they stem from the same place."

"Really?" She didn't want to hear more, but she couldn't seem to keep herself from asking, "Where?"

"You tell me. Close your eyes."

The spoon full of pasty-smelling cereal froze in midair. Hannah's hand trembled slightly.

"Close your eyes," Aunt Phiz urged again, this time slipping the spoon from Hannah's hand and taking up the task of feeding Tessa herself.

Hannah swallowed. If she leapt up now and pretended she had to go, she might make her getaway. But get away from what? Independence and insecurities stemmed from the same place—within her. No matter how fast she ran, she'd never get away from that.

So she obeyed her aunt and shut her eyes.

"Your fear that nobody wants you and your need to prove that you don't need anybody come from…" She took Hannah's hand and waited for her to finish.

"My mother's leaving." No surprise there. Then why did the hurt of saying it feel so fresh?

"Honey, she's been gone all your life. Isn't it time you finally found a way to make peace with that? With her? With yourself?"

"I've tried. And every time I think I just may have done it—"

"Knock, knock!" A woman's voice wafted through the house from the front door.

Aunt Phiz flinched, then started to lumber up from her chair. "That's the neighbor lady. I'll send her on and stay and take care of Tessa."

"Phyllis? Just poking my head in to say I got all the way over here and forgot my glasses. I'll be right back."

Phiz turned to call out, but Hannah stopped her.

"It's okay. You made these plans long before I sprang this Tessa deal on you."

"But you deserve some time alone to deal with the destroy-it-yourself sisters and maybe do a bit of soul-searching."

Soul-searching? Destroy-it-yourself? Hannah shuddered to hear them both so closely phrased together. "No, thanks, Aunt Phiz. You get your hair done. Tessa can tag along with me this time."

"Or you could pack your bags and fly away."

"What?"

"Don't you remember?"

Hannah rolled her eyes. Of course she remembered.

But Aunt Phiz was going to tell it anyway. "When you girls were little, I'd come and stay as often as possible. But my work made demands. And there were those times when my husbands were still alive and expected the wifey to put in the odd appearance at home."

"Odd appearance. Have you ever made any other kind?" Hannah chuckled kindly.

"I'd like to think that sometimes I made a welcome appearance?"

"Yes." She could still recall the excitement that ruled

their house when word came that their aunt had scheduled a visit. "But then you always had to…you always had to fly away."

"And you used to ask if you could come."

Hannah shut her eyes again. She took in a deep breath, and with it the familiar scent of tea and baby food and home. "Pack me in your bag, Aunt Phiz, and fly me away with you."

"I'd do it now if I could, but you're too big to fit in my bag." She touched the tip of Hannah's nose. "And you have your own husband and family expecting you to make the odd appearance around the house."

"True, and right now I have two sisters who want me to appear at the church in a few minutes—only I won't be the odd one in that scenario."

"One phone call and I can cancel my hair."

"Oh, no, Aunt Phiz. How could I ever live with myself if I were the cause of you canceling your hair?" Hannah smiled, kissed her aunt on the cheek and started taking the baby out of her high chair.

"The baby won't get in the way?"

Hannah pressed her lips to the child's chubby, cereal-slimed cheek. "Never. Besides, it's just two very well-intentioned women slapping some paint on a nursery wall. Nothing I can't handle. Nothing we can't handle together—right, Tessa?"

The baby giggled.

"What a happy, happy girl you are!" Hannah cooed. "Ready to go out and take on the world?"

Tessa kicked her legs and laughed some more.

Hannah had barely gotten the first hint of chuckle out when the smell hit her.

"Looks like before we take on the world, we have to make some big changes. And it won't be pleasant." She just hoped that wasn't an indication of what the rest of the day held for her.

12

Subject: Nacho Mama's House column
To: Features@Wileyvillenews.com
Police tape.

In a great big yellow X across the doors of both the baby and toddler rooms!

I'll give you a moment to visualize. (Checking my watch. Humming.) Got it? Okeydoke, now let me ask you something in all sincerity.

Two sisters working together day in and day out, yet never seeming to get any closer to their goal. One morning you arrive to find the scene of their collaboration cordoned off by police tape. What would you think?

Sister-cide, right? Or whatever it's called when female sibs have finally had enough and turn on each other with whatever weapons they have at their disposal.

Thank the Lord all the girls could lay hands on were paint rollers and caulk guns. Jacqui will never get that stuff out of her hair. Cydney's self-designed clothes now have a nifty new color to them—Canary. And as for the nursery suite…

It's curtains for the window treatments. Dirt knap for the carpets. And Noah's Ark is sleeping with the fishes.

Trust me, in this case police tape is a vast improvement.

Not official police tape. No crime committed. No names changed to protect the innocent. This bright yellow-and-black plastic caution tape came from one of those megasize home improvement stores. I'm thinking of wrapping both rooms in it, handing the minister the keys and walking away.

Of course, that won't work. Everyone knows where I live.

Sister-cide. I can't lie—something akin to it has crossed my mind. But today I am counting my blessings that in all our many adventures from childhood on, my sisters and I have never tried to work together on anything more demanding than rescuing Daddy from another wayward adventure.

—From Nacho Mama's House column

"Daddy did what?" Hannah pressed her cell phone to one ear and put her finger in the other. And she still couldn't hear her sister over the bickering of the DIY sisters. Tessa wailed. A freshly primped and permed Aunt Phiz who had run to the rescue when Hannah called to report the mess sang as she worked loose the corner of the paint-spattered carpet. "He said what to who?"

"What?" Phiz jerked her head up. "What's that baby brother of mine gone and done now?"

"Baby?" Jacqui stopped wagging her finger in her sister's face long enough to send a disbelieving look at Hannah's elderly spitfire of an aunt.

"Yes. *Baby* brother." To the dauntless Phyllis Amaryllis, Moonie Shelnutt was and always would be her sweet "baby" sibling, even though they were both well into collecting Social Security.

"If only I had been blessed with a baby brother instead of a bossy sister." Jacqui finger-combed her hair, only to hit a snarl of still-moist caulk mixed with paint. She groaned and drew her hand away.

Hannah and Phiz both saw what was coming, but they couldn't warn Cydney fast enough to stop her frantic spit-cleaning of her tennis shoe and duck.

Th-wapp!

"Oh!" Cydney took the lightly flung goop right across the cheek. "Why you—"

"Watch your mouth. We're in the church, *baby* sister."

Cydney narrowed her eyes and swiped the mess off with the back of her hand. "Better to *be* the baby than to *act* like the baby."

"Shh, *ladies!*" And she meant that term in the most lenient sense possible. "Please! I can't listen to you, quiet my baby and talk to Sadie all at the same time."

If only God had blessed her with that level of multitasking! Maybe then she'd finally get everything done and make everyone happy all at once. She picked Tessa up from the baby seat on the floor, planted the child on her hip and began pacing.

The noise level dropped to a dull roar.

Hannah shut her eyes to blot out everything but her sister's voice. "Say that again, Sadie. Daddy went where and asked for what?"

"He went into the vet clinic with his neighbor's new kitten tucked under his arm and announced, 'I'm here for my cat scan!'"

Maybe it was the ridiculousness of her situation. Or maybe having the image form in her head of her daddy clutching a small furball to his blue sweater, his gray hat screwed down tight to hide the orneriness in his eyes that set her off. Hannah didn't know. And it didn't matter. She had to laugh.

"Great fun for you, sure." Sadie's bristling carried like an electrical current through the lines.

"Besides, if anyone is acting infantile around here, maybe we should look to the person whose immature artistic style belongs stuck up on a refrigerator, not factored into a design scheme." Jacqui shook her head to loosen more caulk.

"Did I catch you at a bad time?" Sadie asked.

"Yes." Hannah moved to the doorway that separated the two rooms. "You did. Excuse me just a second."

She caught Jacqui by the arm and helped her through to the next room, where her sister stood surveying the wreckage that had once been a pair of hand-decorated shoes.

"Jacqui? Cydney? This is an important phone call. It's concerning my family. For the next few minutes, all issues concerning my family will be being conducted over there." She pointed to the toddler room. "All issues concerning *your* family will be contained in here."

Wham. She slammed the door between herself and the wide-eyed, paint-slopped sisters.

"But then, there doesn't seem to be such a thing as a good time to catch me these days," she told her own sister in the sweetest tone imaginable. "So go on talking."

"Okay. So Daddy pulls this stunt at the vet, and after the giggling died down in the waiting room, he tells everyone there to be sure to let his busybody daughter know that he'd reported for his test as per her orders."

"Did he now?"

"I've been fielding calls all day long."

"Interesting."

"Interesting that Daddy pulled this stunt, or interesting that he actually listened to what I told him and acted on it—childishly—but acted on it just the same?"

"Interesting that when told to get word to his *busybody* daughter, everyone called *you*."

Sadie chuckled soft and quick before clucking her tongue. "I guess if he'd said call his celebrity daughter, you'd be the one trying to convince Lollie Mulldoon that Daddy's actions sprang from sarcasm, not a desperate plea for help."

"Sarcasm? What's prompted Daddy to resort to sarcasm now?"

"Not like he needs prompting." Aunt Phiz and Sadie treated Hannah to the remark in stereo.

Hannah blinked.

Aunt Phiz suddenly got terribly involved in not looking like she'd been eavesdropping. She gave the far corner of the carpet a mighty yank.

A long, ominous ripping sound tore through the vacant room as the flooring came loose.

Sadie pressed on. "What usually leads him to sarcasm? He's trying to take the heat off."

"The heat off?"

"Because he doesn't want to have the tests."

"Oh."

Hannah rubbed her forehead, but that didn't ease the tension brought on by the reminder of their father's transient ischemic attacks. He had the first about the time she'd learned she was pregnant with Tessa. The same time they had all learned about the ultimate, heartbreaking fate of their mother.

"What?" The carpet fell from Aunt Phiz's grip, sending a load of musty-smelling dust through the room.

Hannah bounced Tessa on her hip, turning away so she wouldn't show her disappointment and concern to her aunt as she answered the question. "The tests."

"He still hasn't gone for those?"

Hannah shook her head.

Payt had tried to hook Daddy up with the best neurologists in Kentucky for a year now, but the old man always had an excuse to cancel the appointments.

"He says he feels fine," Hannah relayed to her aunt.

"Let's just see if he's still saying that once I get a hold of him." The old gal slapped her hands together. Her ample upper arms swayed and joggled, making her look pretty formidable for a senior citizen with a clown-hair-colored poodle perm.

"You?" Hannah asked.

"Who?" Sadie shot back.

"Me!" Phiz motioned for Hannah to hand her the small cell phone. "Sounds like our Sadie has her hands full. And since you don't seem ready or willing to accept my help, why shouldn't I hie myself down to Wileyville to see what I can do?"

Because you're my help. You came to me. To impose yourself on my life. Not Sadie's. Mine.

Mine, mine, mine.

Not since Daddy's last stunt had anyone responded with such unreasoned childishness.

At least once a day, maybe more, Hannah secretly wished her aunt would fly back to China or India or even just drive to the drugstore long enough to give Hannah a breather. But hearing her announce her plans to leave, the truth hit Hannah. For once in her life, someone had come running to her first, not to her sisters. If Aunt Phiz ran off to Sadie's aid at this first bit of small trouble, where would that leave Hannah?

Talking to herself. That's where. And it had already been pointed out to her that she was no good at that kind of thing.

Suddenly she felt like the lost, lonely child she had once been. She wished her aunt could pack her up in a suitcase and fly her away.

"Give me the phone, honey." Phiz stuck out her open palm.

"No, wait!" Sadie, who for someone who had the patience of a gnat had gotten pretty good at telling other people to wait, lowered her voice and spoke in a quick, panicked tone. "Tell Aunt Phiz I have things under control. We've finally got the MRI scheduled at a time that I can take him."

Hannah relayed the message word for word.

"I'm hanging up now before she gets a chance to argue. Give her my love." And Sadie was gone.

"Thanks a lot," Hannah muttered. She depressed the end call button with one thumb, then showed the turned-off phone to her aunt with a shrug. "Guess Sadie had to run."

"I'll bet." Aunt Phiz shook her head.

Hannah slid the phone into her purse. She paused to listen for the sisters in the next room. "That's certainly an eerie silence."

"Maybe they've made their peace."

"Maybe they're resting in peace. If you know what I mean." She stuck her tongue out and made a slash across her throat with one finger.

Tessa grabbed her hand in motion and promptly began to gnaw on one knuckle.

"I'd like to go in there and put Tessa in one of the cribs while we finish up in here."

"Stealth, my dear." The older woman raised a penciled-in eyebrow. "Get in, get out, don't get involved."

Hannah nodded. "Good idea."

She took a breath, laid her hand on the door and waited. For what, she didn't know, but that's what they always told you to do in those Safety First filmstrips at school.

Feel the door to prevent walking into a fiery death trap.

No heat.

No sound.

She glanced back at her aunt.

"Go!" Phiz urged.

"Please excuse me for one moment, ladies, but I need to put Tessa…" She had the baby halfway into the crib before she realized she'd been talking to an empty room.

"Where'd they go?" Aunt Phiz asked.

"I don't know and I don't care." Hannah put the baby down and hurried back through to the toddler room. "Let's just finish our work here and run before they get back."

"Yes. Good. When in doubt work fast and get out." Aunt Phiz held up her index finger. "That shall be the new Shelnutt family motto."

Hannah liked it. She liked it a little too much.

In fact, she wished she could have put it into action moments later when she and her aunt stood elbow-deep in dirty work and the older woman turned the subject to Hannah's daddy again.

"MRI, you said?"

"Yes. It's a magnetic resonance imagining machine." Hannah made a motion in the air with her free hand to try to indicate the big tube that they would be sliding Moonie into.

"I know what it is, honey. You might recall I hold multiple advanced degrees in history and science."

"Oh, yeah." *Clod! You did it again. Thought only in terms of yourself and your experience with someone, and ended up missing out on the bigger picture.* "I guess when you see someone everyday in curlers and house slippers, you tend to forget she's a well-educated world traveler. Dopey me."

"You are not dopey. You are darling. And dedicated. And more than a little distracted." Soft folds framed Aunt Phiz's sparkling eyes and kind smile. "But never dopey. Don't tell yourself different."

"Thanks."

"Not only do I know what an MRI is, my dear, I had reason to see one in action a few years back when one of my classes got to observe a mummy being sent through the device."

"Wow." Hannah blinked. "That must have been fascinating."

"Yes, indeed."

"Maybe you can use that story to convince Daddy to give it a try."

"The test of choice for three-thousand-year-old pharaohs?" She tapped her finger to her cheek. "It might just be the thing to appeal to his vanity to know he was in the company of kings."

"If nothing else, it would give him a terrific lead-in for the epic tale of Moonie's Medical Miracle." Hannah dropped to her knees to better roll up the heavy old carpet. "Way better than that taking-the-cat-to-the-vet story."

"I don't think so. After that experience?" Phiz did her bit by nudging the musty cylinder along with her foot. "Not even for the sake of telling a great story will your daddy get inside of one of those closed MRI machines."

"I don't know about that. You've never gone up against Sadie once she's made her mind up."

"She's a stubborn one, I'll give you that. But where do you think all that mule-headedness comes from?"

"Let me guess, from Moonie, the Mule King?"

"Moonie the Miracle Boy."

"Is this the story about how he got lost in a cave and lived on his own for days and everyone gave him up for dead, then miraculously he came wandering out without a scratch on him?"

"Is that how he tells it now?"

"He hasn't talked about it in years and years. I've probably got it all wrong."

"It's worth hearing to get it right. Might help you look at your dad in a new light." The tight coils of bright red hair bounced slightly as she cocked her head. "I'll make it quick if you promise to listen—to really listen."

"Okay." What was it with everyone suddenly picking on her listening skills? "But quick, right? We don't know when the sisterhood of the splattered paint might up and return."

Phiz made a seat of the lump of carpet and patted the spot beside herself for Hannah to join her.

"He couldn't have been more than three. Darling child. Charming. Well, you know how he musters up that spark in his eyes to get himself out of trouble now?"

Know it? Hannah sometimes wondered if it was the reason her mother had run off in the night leaving only a note. How could anyone look into those eyes and still have the strength to walk away?

"Imagine all that charming power in the hands of a rosy-cheeked imp."

Hannah held up her hand. "I've seen the photo of him when he won the beautiful baby contest at the county fair."

Phiz tipped her head back and laughed. "Beautiful baby? Is that what he told you that ribbon was for?"

"Wasn't it?"

"One day I'll tell you about your daddy, a daring escape from a droopy diaper, a mud field and the greased pig contest."

"I'll remind you." And she would. It sounded like something she could definitely use against her father the next time he acted out. "But you wanted to tell me about the Miracle Boy?"

"Yes. Yes. He did not come by that name undeserved."

"He performed a miracle?"

"Darling, he *was* a miracle."

"Beg your pardon?"

"Like I said, he couldn't have been more than three when he wandered off. It was an unusually warm spring day, and our parents were having one of their regular knock-down-drag-out rows."

Hannah crossed her legs at the ankle. She knew her aunt Phiz and her father's childhood was less than idyllic. In fact, she'd often wondered if who they had become—Phiz someone who never stayed put, and Moonie, a man who would do anything in the world to lighten a loved one's day—had sprung from the roots of their dark youth.

"Now, on this particular day, I was supposed to be keeping an eye on Moonie. While, in fact, I was keeping both eyes on Judd Harkner."

Hannah raised her eyebrows.

"Another story for another day," Aunt Phiz demurred. "But on this day, the day I was supposed to be watching

Moonie, I took my eyes off him, and the next thing I know—whoosh."

"Whoosh?"

"Moonie vanished!"

"Vanished?"

"I was near frantic. Judd rounded up the boys, and everyone searched and searched. Afternoon turned into evening. No Moonie."

Hannah's thoughts went to Tessa and Sam. Just the suggestion of them lost and her not able to get to them, to comfort them. A cold, hard lump clenched tight in her chest.

"Got too dark to keep on looking. And cool. Not cold, but too cool for a little child like that left out without any cover. And there was the threat of wild animals." Even all these years later, her old aunt's face went pale. A little shiver worked through her broad body.

"But you found him."

"Honey, of course we found him. You wouldn't be here today to hear this story if we hadn't found him."

"Oh. Of course." Hannah blinked and probably blushed. "Of course."

"It was the prayer vigil that did it."

"Prayer is a powerful thing."

"We have no idea how powerful, girl. We humans are so prideful and shortsighted. We think we can fix every little thing, when we should turn it all over to the Lord."

Hannah nodded. "So you held a prayer vigil."

"We lit candles. Sheltered them in our hands against the evening wind." She cupped a hand around the remembered candle. "And prayed."

She wanted to hurry her aunt along, not out of a need to rush the story but to hear the end, to try to understand what had compelled the woman to tell her this now and what it meant to getting her father the medical tests he needed.

"And then we heard it."

"What?"

"Moonie's voice."

She sighed. "Where was he?"

"Didn't know at first, but we followed the sound. It seemed to come from nowhere and everywhere all at once."

"Wow."

"It was something to experience, I tell you that right now. We couldn't get a handle on where he was until, quite by accident, someone stepped in a hole and tripped."

"He was in the hole."

"He was in a dry well that someone had only partly covered, and when he'd tried to climb out, he'd pulled more dirt and rock down on him until he was all but buried except one arm and his head."

"Poor Daddy."

"Your grandpa dug him out with his bare hands."

"Did it take long?"

"Longer than you might think, because they didn't dare risk the dirt falling back and smothering him."

"I can't imagine it."

"I sat at his side the whole time, holding up a candle and telling him he'd be all right. Telling him not to be afraid. Telling him to have faith."

"Do you think he understood you?"

"On some level, yes, I do. And furthermore, I know he'll understand me now."

"Now?"

"Yes, when I go to sit beside him while he gets that MRI."

"He's…he's claustrophobic. That's the point of the story?"

"The point of the story, Hannah Banana, is you girls may have gotten some things from your daddy. Sadie her stubbornness and that sarcastic streak. And you, your independent spirit and that longing to sometimes fly away and leave your troubles behind."

Hannah folded her arms and tapped her double-knotted sneaker against the carpet backing. "You could have just told me those things outright."

"Yes, but I couldn't have made you understand why I have to go to be with your daddy to get him to take the tests he needs."

"Because his history makes him afraid of closed-in spaces," she reiterated.

"Listen, child." A beaded earring clacked quietly as Phiz turned her head and pointed to her ear. "I'm saying that at some points in our lives we are all frightened children who need God's hands in human form. We need someone we love to remain steadfast beside us no matter what. To hold up the light to show the way."

Hannah shut her eyes and could almost hear her father calling out to the one person he had trusted all those years ago. "To remind us we are not alone."

"And to pray," Phiz whispered.

Hannah opened her eyes and sat up, suddenly aware she'd been leaning on her aunt's ample shoulder. She took one age-spotted hand in hers and met the loving, time-wizened gaze. "How long will you be gone?"

"Will it really matter to you?"

"Of course."

"Good." Phiz lumbered upward to her feet. "I'll leave today. And, Hannah Banana?"

Hannah felt all of five years old again, looking up at her aunt who was about to leave again. "What?"

"When you're ready, when you're *really* ready for my help, you call out. I'll come back so fast it will make your head spin."

"Well, I'll just take that up with Hannah, if you don't mind." Cydney's voice echoed in the stairwell.

"I don't mind one bit, because I know she will definitely be on my side." Jacqui could not have been more than a footfall behind.

"That's not so hot a trick." Hannah staggered to her feet and gave the carpet one gigantic heave. "Everyday life makes my head spin, Aunt Phiz."

13

Subject: Nacho Mama's House column
To: Features@Wileyvillenews.com
When you're tired and you can't sleep—you're probably at my house.

End of soccer season. Now there's an oxymoron if I ever heard one. Soccer season has no end. It just has brief pauses for the kids to regain their strength. Between indoor and outdoor leagues, and programs provided by the parks department, private clubs—not to mention the school team—a kid could literally play soccer any time but in his sleep.

And listening to the racket coming from my living room, some of them even try to play it then. In their sleep. Or should I say "alleged sleep." It's what they're supposed to be doing, according to the front of the invites we sent out. Come to an End of Soccer Season Sleepover.

Sleepover? Sleepover?

Want to talk oxymoron? I'll sit and hum quietly to myself while you insert your own moron joke about this new-to-motherhood mom who actually thought when a bunch of eight- and nine-year-old boys showed up at her house with sleeping bags that they intended to crawl in them and catch some Z's. Yeah, at a sleepover.

No. Nuh-uh. No way. No sleep. No over. At this point it doesn't feel like it will ever be over.

Other than that...

I'm just sitting here quietly counting my blessings—starting with chocolate and earplugs.

—From Nacho Mama's House column

"'Ten little monkeys jumping on the bed.'" Hannah held her finger up and moved it up and down to demonstrate the rhyme for Tessa.

The baby's head bobbed slightly following along. She sucked her fist.

Teething.

"Let's look on the bright side, baby girl, at least you picked a night when I hadn't figured on getting any sleep anyway to cut your first tooth."

Cries of "Stilton's turn" and "Go for it, Stilton" rose from the front room sleepover encampment.

"I should go see about that." Hannah started to push up from the rocker.

"Gross!"

"Ee-uw!"

She fell back down into the seat and set it swaying back and forth again. "Maybe I'll hold off on that a while."

She pressed the pad of her thumb to her daughter's lower lip to steal a peek at her teething progress.

Tessa ground her pink gums together and made a cranky growling sound.

"I couldn't agree more." Hannah rubbed her knuckle over the milky white tooth bud just below the swollen surface.

Tessa nestled down deeper into her mother's arms and let out a shuddering breath.

Hannah kissed her daughter's temper-fit-dampened red curls and went on with the singsonged tale of monkeys misbehaving. "'Mama called the doctor and the doctor said—'"

"Hannah, tell those boys to quiet down. I had a long day at work."

She glared out the door of her daughter's room, imagining she had some kind of laser vision that would turn the corner and travel along the dark hallway through the keyhole and find her husband lying in the cozy, rumpled bed.

"I love your daddy more than I could ever express, but honestly, Tessa, darling, sometimes he can be such a…a…a man."

Tessa's expression soured. She growled again.

"Uh-huh. You tell it like it is, girl."

"Hannah? Please! Are you going to handle this?"

Deal with it? Tempting. Very tempting to holler back her opinion of him yelling at her to yell at the boys to stop yelling so he could have quiet.

That or she could just resign herself to the inevitable and deal directly with the boys. Either way, voices would get raised with not much chance of reaching the desired result.

She clenched her jaw. She pressed the side of Tessa's head close, then covered the baby's delicate exposed ear with one hand.

Tessa drooled down the front of both her and Hannah's nightgowns.

Deep breath. Time to assert herself. "Let's show a little consideration, please."

There. Somebody in this house ought to respond to *that*.

"Yes, ma'am," a blend of childish voices chimed back.

Not so much as a peep from Payt.

One shove of her foot set Hannah's rocking chair in motion again. "He had a long day. Did you hear that, Tessa?"

The baby snuggled close, and Hannah drew in the comforting scent of powder and warm baby's breath.

"*Our* day isn't over yet, is it? Not to mention that we know exactly how long his day was…and why."

She shut her eyes….

"You're cool with that, aren't you, Hannah?" She could picture her husband standing by the front door to his office at precisely twenty-eight minutes past four.

She knew the time practically right down to the last tick of the second hand, because she'd worried that dragging Sam, Tessa and a tub of cleaning supplies into his office, even a few minutes before they locked the doors might embarrass him in front of his patients.

"Um, I suppose—"

"See? She's cool with it." Dr. Briggs punched Payt in the arm. Hard.

Payt made a noise—not quite a laugh, not really a cough.

Dr. Briggs barked out a belly laugh. He was taller than Hannah had remembered him. Maybe he'd been sitting those times? But that didn't explain how she'd missed the jovial expression and soft white wavy hair. He looked like some moon-faced gentle giant straight out of a children's picture book.

It made it all the more difficult to hang on to her reservations about the man. Until he opened his mouth.

"Tell you what, Bartlett, you got yourself a real jewel there. If my second wife had understood the demands of a doctor's life the way Hannah does, maybe she'd still be my wife." He gave Dottie, the office manager, a wink as he pushed past her toward the door.

"If his wife had understood any more about that man's demands, she'd be his widow." Dottie raised both hands and made a choking motion in midair, then rolled her eyes.

Payt bent at the knees to put his face low enough to look up into Hannah's eyes. "You really okay with this?" he asked.

She heard: *Do you really want to still be my wife?*

"I…I understand, Payt." Dr. Briggs had made it clear she had no choice.

Listen to yourself! You're taking someone else's words and putting them in Payt's mouth. Don't turn every innocent comment into a club to beat yourself up with. You always assume the worst.

"That's not really an answer." Her husband stroked her cheek. His eyes searched hers, and for a moment she thought maybe he wanted her to tell him not to go.

That only made it harder for her. If she knew what he wanted her to say, she'd say it.

"Just tell me how you feel about this, okay?"

"I feel…silly. It's silly. Go." *Don't go.*

"Yeah?"

"Have fun." *But not too much fun.*

"But I feel so guilty leaving you here to do the cleaning."

"Why? I said I'd do it until you get the—" she glanced around to make sure no one else could hear "—the scapegoat issue settled. And seeing as how it's Heather's birthday—well, how could I object to you going to dinner to show your support?"

Really. How? She wished he would stand right there and tell her word for word how to object, what to say to not sound petty and small, to maintain her dignity and keep her husband at her side.

He slipped his name tag off his shirt pocket and tossed it onto Heather's desk with the clutter of birthday cards and icing-smeared napkins. "We would have done it at lunch, but these sales reps had something planned for her, and we couldn't just close up and take off."

"I know." She pulled a smile up from someplace in her being. "The demands of a doctor's life."

"Thanks for being so—"

Wishy-washy, she wanted to say. Instead she finished for him, "Understanding."

"I won't be too late." He kissed her temple.

"Maybe you already are," she murmured as she watched him breeze out the door to some restaurant where energetic waiters wrote their names on the table-cloth and peppered the snappy recitation of the specials with their own hyperhappy recommendations. "I could live on the double-stuffed crab cakes with mango salsa!"

Ugh.

Payt went off to double-stuff himself, while she had to stay and clean the staff restroom.

Classic Cinderella syndrome. She'd had it all her life.

But it wasn't supposed to be like this. Not a Christian marriage. Not her marriage. She wasn't supposed to feel neglected, as if she would always come in second place.

Not that it was a new sensation. Second-place sister. She'd felt it all her life whenever someone gushed over the accomplishments of Sadie or April. Hannah, the runner-up. The one they only went to when their first choice had other plans.

She'd felt that way in school, in matters dealing with their daddy and almost every minute of the years she spent working and living in Wileyville while Payt put in his time at the clinic there.

In those places she expected it. But not in her own marriage.

She set the rocker moving again. Eyes open in the dimly lit baby's room, she let her gaze flit from one familiar object to another, thinking of what it all represented.

All the years of planning and hoping.

All the time invested in creating a home, a relationship, a future.

Everything they had gone through to become a family, and where had she ended up?

Alone.

Excluded. Only for an evening, but still… Her own husband had abandoned her to go celebrate another woman's birthday, while Hannah stayed to clean up the partygoers' trash.

In her marriage she expected…

"Honesty," she whispered. She'd always thought that no matter what else, she and Payt had that. Honesty.

Had she learned differently today?

She hadn't meant to snoop. No. No one could call it snooping.

She hadn't gone there on some kind of wifely fact-finding mission, after all. Payt had roped her into cleaning his office.

"It isn't my fault he hung himself with that rope," Hannah murmured.

Tessa waved her dripping wet fist in the air, bonking Hannah on the chin.

"Yes. Yes. Right. Too melodramatic." Hannah laughed, sort of. The she sighed and shook her head. "Get used to it, darling. Your mom has a knack for taking the smallest ambiguous seed of doubt and turning it into a great big jungle garden of anxiety."

Tessa poked her fingers into her mouth again.

"Your mama never seems too busy to get away for a guilt trip." Hannah nuzzled her daughter's warm cheek. "And your daddy…according to the notation on your daddy's desk calendar, your daddy is going to Miami. In ten days. And he has yet to say a word to me about it."

Saying it out loud took her breath away. Miami.

"Miami?" Maybe he meant Little Miami River Park? She tried to imagine Payt having a meeting at one of the spots in the park not too far from their home in Loveland. No. It didn't fit. The word she had seen had nothing to do with the river of the same name. Miami.

Tessa kicked and fussed and kicked some more. She moved her head to a cool dry spot on Hannah's chest and sighed.

Hannah exhaled with her child. "There's probably a perfectly sound reason for it. Something we'll both laugh about when he tells me about it."

If he told her.

He'd have to tell her.

"I mean, the man can be oblivious, but even he would

understand that if he just took off for Florida, I'd notice his absence."

Tessa yawned.

Hannah yawned, too. "Okay, putting this in perspective, this will all seem much less of a big deal after a good night's sleep."

A hushed roar rolled in from the boys in the front room, followed by a shower of "shhs" and sundry other shushing sounds.

"I bet your daddy will explain everything to me in the morning."

Wouldn't he?

She got to her feet and, patting Tessa on the back, walked to the crib. "'One little monkey jumping on the bed. He fell off and bumped his head. Mama called the doctor, and the doctor said…'"

14

Subject: Nacho Mama's House column
To: Features@Wileyvillenews.com
Good riddance to bad rubbish.

Rubbish? Sound a bit harsh?

Come to the toddler and baby rooms of my little church, look long and hard at the aftermath of the DI-why-oh-why-did-I-let-them-talk-me-into-this? Duo's efforts to fix what they destroyed, and you tell me. I think rubbish might be too kind.

When they heard about my father's impending tests (Hi, Daddy! Hope someone is reading this to you while you get that open MRI done) and my aunt wanting to go to him, they felt really bad about the way they acted. Bad enough that they promised on the spot to work together tirelessly until they had put everything right. And if you have a sister that you have worked with for two months on a project, only to see it end in paint-shed, well, you know just how sincerely terrible they felt to make that pledge.

And they tried, bless their hearts, they did try. But I think we all learned the hard way that not all of the things you see done on TV home décor shows work in real life. Sewing children's cast-off sweaters together does not make all that attractive a throw rug—though it did live up to the name. I certainly wanted to throw the thing right out the window. So we'll get by sans the makeshift replacement for the ugly rug.

As for rescuing the rest of the project?

No matter how much Jacqui and Cydney dabbed and rag-rolled and patched the wallpaper, we finally had to face the facts. Their well-intentioned redo would simply have to be redone.

So here I am spending my Saturday at the church, stripping wallpaper and trying to sink Noah's Ark (aka the mural of a gray, shoe-shaped boat populated by green and blue and pink animals with enormous toothy smiles). The man at the paint store recommended I first use something to "kill" the clash of color instead of doing multiple coats.

"I don't know," I said. "This is for a church and we follow the Commandment Thou Shall Not Kill."

The paint guy didn't laugh, either.

He just asked how many gallons I needed and in what color.

Payt suggested yellow. Studies show that yellow energizes the mind and body. Think about that. A room filled with two- and three-year-olds, energized in mind and body. What do those studies find works best for inducing drowsiness?

Aunt Phiz, in a call from Wileyville—where she is still staying because her baby brother is acting every bit the part and sopping up her attention like a biscuit in greasy gravy—says to use bold colors and geometric shapes. To stimulate creativity. Just what I need. Toddlers with the mental capacity to form complex escape plans using blocks and tippy cups.

Nope. Much as I appreciate the well-considered suggestions, I have settled on the paint color that I think best suits the current situation.

Eggshell.

You know, as in what I am constantly walking on trying to please everyone?

It's perfect.

—From "Nacho Mama's House" column

"What were we thinking here, Hannah?"

We? She had heard of the royal "we." And had worked with an old-style doctor or two who still insisted on walking into a patient's room and asking, "How are we feeling today?" But coming from the mouth of their bright-eyed young minister in his fisherman's knit sweater and custom-made-for-fall corduroy pants, it riled Hannah's suspicions. Just who were "we" and what were "we" supposed to think?

She found no answer in his broad face.

"*I'm* thinking, Reverend Tappin…" She'd been thinking how much she missed Aunt Phiz. How even though school and friends took up more and more of *Sam's* day, she didn't seem to have more time in *her* day. And on top of that, she missed the kid. And Payt.

He hadn't said a word about Miami. She'd hoped to ask him this morning, but how could she with a houseful of boys in pajamas and boxes of colored cereal spilled on her table and all the moms about to converge on her house to pick up their boys? And with her commitment to come to the church and repaint…

Oh. Paint. That was the topic at hand. She stepped back and took in the serene, calming neutrality of the blank wall. "We're thinking…that it's perfect?"

"I'm thinking—" he tilted his head like a man trying to make sense of modern art "—that it looks exactly like it did before you started this renovation project two months ago."

"No. Not at all." Easy fix. Just point out the obvious and get out of the way. "Before, the walls had this dingy, not-quite-white thing going."

"And now?"

She swept her arm out with the grace of a practiced spokesmodel. "Eggshell."

He cleared his throat.

"Eggshell," she reiterated, adding extra oomph to the motion of her outstretched arm.

"You know, Hannah…"

Not good. No one started good news off with "You know, Hannah…"

"I've been doing some thinking myself." He scratched his fingers through his short blond hair, leaving a rooster tail on top.

"Oh?" She smoothed her hand along the top of her own head, hoping he'd pick up on the hint.

"I have." He didn't exactly frown. But his expression did take on a decisive does-this-milk-taste-funny-to-you? quality. "It's not that I don't appreciate all your effort and hard work on behalf of the nursery program. But…"

But?

She swallowed and touched her chilled fingers to her throat. The man planned to fire her. For something that wasn't technically her fault.

Fired? From a volunteer position?

Worse! From a volunteer position she had written about extensively in her weekly newspaper column! Taking rejection was one thing. She'd taken that all her life. In fact, she'd taken on far more rejection than she had actually received. All those imagined slights, the overblown reactions, the hurts borrowed against her ever-present fear that someone would not like her.

But this…this would go too far. This she could not suppress with a shaky smile. Everyone would know about this.

"I know it doesn't look like much of an improvement, Reverend." In fact, looking close now, she could see the product designed to kill the other paint colors had left a few ghosts behind. She turned her back to the wall. "But I was dealt circumstances beyond my control—that got beyond my control—that went entirely out of control—"

"Don't worry, dear." He laid a comforting hand on her shoulder. "The first wedding I ever performed in this church? A world-exclusive Jacqui Lafferty and Cydney Snowden Technicolor extravaganza."

Her shoulders sank in relief, and she breathed out a sigh and an almost inaudible "Thank you."

He nodded.

As an afterthought—and she did feel more than a little guilty that it didn't spring to her mind sooner—she added, "But please don't hold any hard feelings toward the ladies. I took the reins of this wild ride, and when I did, took on all the responsibility for the nursery and toddler department. I may have let this redecorating business get out of hand, but let me assure you that from now you can count on me to keep my ducks in a row."

"Ducks?" He jutted his square chin out. "Funny you should mention those."

Because you look just like one in that fluffy sweater, downy ruffle of blond hair and sticking your chin out like that? One blessing of the driving desire to make everybody love her—she didn't say half the stuff that popped into her head.

"Because what I've been thinking was not about ducks. More like how do you think you'd manage with doves?"

"Doves?" she cooed.

"And sheep?"

"Sheep?" she bleated.

"And camels?"

"I'm sorry, but did you say—?"

He nodded. "Camels."

She tried to swallow, but her throat had gone dry as the desert. "I—I don't know how I'd manage any of those. It would be like playing zookeeper."

"Or innkeeper," he murmured, his smile breaking slowly.

"Innkeeper?"

"Or innkeeper's wife, more precisely. It's not mandatory, but we've found Innkeeper's Wife is an ideal part to grant total access to the stage."

"The, uh, stage?"

"The best vantage point to oversee things, you'd have to agree."

"I would?"

"Without the demands of memorizing lines. I assume you wouldn't want that?"

"Demands? No, I prefer to avoid demands whenever possible."

"So, it's the Innkeeper's Wife, then?"

"For?"

"You, Hannah. That or Stable Man—Stable Person, I guess, in your case."

Stable Person. She supposed she should consider it a kind of compliment that someone would string those two words together to refer to her. Even if that person was using that string to tie her into knots! "Reverend Tappin, surely you're not asking me to—"

"Take charge of the children's Christmas pageant. Yes, Hannah, it's yours if you want it."

"But after the redecorating—the chaos, the confusion, the cost—only to end up looking just like it did before I started." She flattened her hand against the shadow of an elephant's face lurking beneath her meticulous Eggshell surface. "Don't you think that shows... something?"

"Indeed I do."

She exhaled in gratitude.

"It shows that you can handle stressful situations."

"I don't think so."

"And cope with childish behavior."

"Uh-uh!"

He laughed, and with one fell swoop whisked his hair back into place. Unruffled. The word fit him at this moment in more ways than one as he said, "Hannah, you don't have to do this."

"Oh." He didn't want her? "Uh, thank you."

"After all, Jacqui and Cydney are probably free."

She gave him a sidelong glance.

No, he wouldn't guilt her into rushing to the rescue.

Not this time.

Really.

"I'd only make a mess of it."

"I seriously doubt that, Hannah, but if you don't feel led to participate this year, we understand."

"We" again. Suddenly she got it. We—the church, her community, people who looked to her to pull her weight around this place.

"I'm so sorry. But Sam and Tessa, you know, they need me."

"Of course." He gave her a quick pat on the back, turned and in passing wrapped one knuckle on the freshly painted wall. "You're right. This covered the old stuff perfectly. Great choice."

Don't you dare.

She clenched her jaw and watched the stout fellow striding down the hallway away from her.

"The kids need me," she called after him. "Everyone is counting on me. If I thought my family could spare me for the time it would take to do it up right, I'd go for it." She snapped her fingers. "Like that."

"Then do it." Payt's hand closed over her raised hand.

"Wha— Payt!" She spun around and bumped heads with her sweet but sneaky hubby.

"Ow." He plastered his hand across his forehead.

She did likewise. "Serves you right for creeping up the back stairs to scare me like that. What are you doing here?"

"Arriving in the nick of time, apparently."

"To do what?"

"To make sure you don't miss out on doing whatever you were just shouting about."

"Running the Christmas pageant."

"Perfect."

"How so?"

"Because you are bright, talented and great with kids."

"Oh, yeah, great with feeding them junk food and getting it all over the house and even getting part of the house in the junk food."

"Hannah…"

"Yeah, yeah, listen to myself. I heard. Now *you* listen to me, Bartlett. I told Reverend Tappin I can't do the pageant because I have to take care of my own kids."

"Then take care of them—and take them with you."

"Payt, I…" She let her voice trail off and she shook her head.

"Give Sam a part."

She froze midshake.

"Given the size of your talent pool, every kid in the church will have a part, right?"

"I suppose they'd have to, except the babies like Tessa. Wait a minute, where is Tessa?"

"Mrs. Tappin grabbed her from me the second I hit the door. Sam went over to Stilton's. All kids accounted for, so you can take a break from worrying."

"Oh." Take a break from worrying? Had the man lost his mind?

"Put the kids out of your thoughts."

He was out of his mind.

"And answer this one question for me."

"Answer a question? That I can do."

"This pageant thing, you wouldn't start working on it right away, would you?"

"I don't know. Why?"

"Because I have a project I want you to start first."

"What?"

"A second honeymoon."

"Miami!"

"Yes! Mi—how'd you know that?"

"Oh, Payt, sometimes you can be such a *man*."

"What's that supposed to mean?"

"It means you made these plans, and it never occurred to you that while you might be able to keep a secret from your wife, you could never keep one from your cleaning lady."

"You saw the notation on my desk."

"And it's been killing me not to tackle you, hold you down and make you tell me about it."

"Really?" He arched an eyebrow. "Maybe I'll just keep the details to myself a little longer then."

She cuddled close to his side and kissed his cheek. "Behave now. We're in church."

"Okay." He held up his hands. "I'm the picture of chaste restraint. For now." He winked. "So, what do you say? Do you want to go to Miami?"

"Want to? *Have* to. All my life I've waited for this, for someone to come along and fly me away. But…"

"No buts. Whatever your reservations, we'll work them out."

Miami. Just like the paint she'd used to cover up the mess and mistakes she'd allowed to happen in this room, this trip would help her create a clean slate.

"Hannah? Hannah, what are you thinking?"

"I'm thinking…" She threw her arms around her husband and said, "I think it's perfect."

She sniffled and blinked the tears from her eyes just as she noticed the faint outline of Noah's Ark beneath the coat of Eggshell.

15

Subject: Nacho Mama's House column
To: Features@Wileyvillenews.com
Sam is on a mission,
The dog is under the bed.
Tessa is in the laundry basket.
And I'm in over my head.
La la.
No, not really. I haven't actually gone off the deep end—yet. But the Christmas pageant planning committee doesn't meet for another two weeks, so give me time!

That's not a complaint. Or a prediction. In fact, for the first time in quite a while, I can honestly say that getting dragged into another responsibility I'll likely mess up has definitely had some positive effects.

For one thing, it's Christmastime in the Bartlett household. Too early for most reasonable people, I realize, though you'd never know it by the store displays of trees and plastic light-up yard figures! But how can I complain when my son, who until now had a pretty shaky grasp on the miracle of Christ's birth, suddenly started practicing all the parts of the Nativity story that might be played by a little boy equipped with a terry-cloth head covering and his father's striped bathrobe?

Moreover, Sam wants to include the whole household in this newfound wonder, from Squirrelly Girl (thus the hiding, because fawn-colored greyhounds are just one sweat jacket—properly stuffed and cinched on to form a hump—away from looking like perfect camels, you know) to Tessa. Yes, my lavender-colored laundry basket is now a makeshift manger bed.

I guess the cliché should embarrass me but there really is nothing like seeing Christmas through a child's eyes. My child's eyes.

Sappy, huh?

Well, we're all allowed our moments. Especially around this place, where nothing seems to hold that sweet sentiment for long.

NOTE TO SELF: FINISH COLUMN BEFORE SENDING

"Oh, no you don't!" Hannah reached down into the laundry basket to retrieve something black-and-white and dripping in baby drool. "Sam, did you give your little sister a dog toy to chew on?"

"Yes!" he called from inside Payt's walk-in closet, where he'd gone to plumb the depths for a silk necktie. Silk neckties, he informed her, make awesome sashes.

"Squirrelly's toy is the only thing that'll quiet her down!" he hollered loud and clear.

He had a point. Even now the baby, who moments ago had lain there contentedly gnawing on the rubber toy made to look like a rolled-up newspaper, coughed and sputtered like an outboard motor gearing up to roar.

"She has teething rings in the freezer. Please go get one for me. I've tried three times now to go out and get the mail and something always—"

R-r-r-r-ring!

"Interrupts me," she muttered under her breath. Dog chew tucked under her arm, she headed for the phone.

"Here. I'm done with this for now." Sam swept by in a blur, pausing only long enough to shove Payt's bathrobe into her arms and to hold up a red silk tie. "If that's Payt on the phone, will you ask him if I can use this for my next costume?"

"Shepherds didn't wear ties," she shouted after him. Unable to dash to the closet to hang it up, and glad for the comfort of something of Payt's around her, she shrugged the robe over her then she reached for the receiver.

"I'm working on a wise-guy costume now."

"Wise men," she corrected. "And I'll ask him, but he may not be in a very good mood."

"Aww, you can cheer him up. You cheer everyone up."

Her hand froze over the phone. That was the nicest thing anyone had said to her today. Today? She could hardly remember the last time anyone had taken time to share a kind word about her efforts. Just: *Here you go, Hannah. We know you won't mind,* and off they go.

How corny did it make her feel that a simple *You can cheer him up. You cheer everyone up* got to her?

Cornier than a whole case of nacho chips. But she didn't care.

Hannah swallowed to push down the emotion welling up from her chest. Now all she had to do was live up to the compliment. Cheery.

Right.

R-r-r-r-ring.

Oh, why not? It probably *was* Payt. They'd waited for him to return her call all afternoon long. She gave her hair a shake, inched her chin up and answered the phone at last. "Nacho Mama's house, the big cheese speaking."

"Hannah? Is that you?"

"Um, Jacqui?"

"And Cydney—patched from my line. Just like a real-live big-business conference call!" the other sister piped in. "Have you got a minute?"

A howl of utter frustration rose from Tessa in the other room. But before Hannah could beg off to go and see about her child, Sam's helpfulness genes kicked in full force. Helpfulness with a little self-serving-brownie-point-grabbing-ness thrown in for good measure.

"I'll take this freezing cold teething thing—carried in my own bare hands, which are also freezing now, but I don't mind—to Tessa, so you can keep talking on the phone!" He went up on tiptoe as he passed, to aim his booming voice directly at the mouthpiece.

Hannah shut her eyes, but not before she glimpsed the grin that all but screamed—*Now Payt can't help but say yes to my borrowing his tie.*

She moved her lips into what she hoped looked more smile than grimace and motioned for the boy to hurry on.

"Guess we have our answer right there." Jacqui laughed.

One beat later Cydney joined in.

Hannah mustered up a weak chuckle, then cleared her throat. "How can I help you ladies today?"

"Wrong question," Jacqui chirped.

Cydney made a grating "you lose" sound like an annoying game show buzzer.

If Cydney had more to contribute than obnoxious sound effects, Jacqui didn't wait for it. "You want to know what you should be asking, Hannah?"

"I…uh…" Hannah shivered. Not from cold, though it had turned cool and cloudy this October afternoon. "Hold on a second, Jacqui."

For good measure, she decided to steel herself against the chill, real or perceived, and wrap herself in Payt's robe. The metaphorical arms of the man poised to whisk her away from all this.

Shifting the receiver from her left ear to her right as she

fumbled to slide her arms into the wide sleeves, she got it on and crammed the dog toy into the deep pockets.

There. Ready. Ready as she'd ever be. "Okay, Jacqui, what question should I be asking?"

"Not 'What can I do for you?' Oh, no."

"No, no, no, no." Cydney's voice took up where Jacqui's left off. "You should be asking—"

"I started all this, Cyd." Jacqui did a quick verbal nudge to push Cydney out of the way and conclude by herself. "What you should be asking, Hannah, is 'What can *you* do for *me?*'"

Heat rose in Hannah's cheeks. She tried to speak, but her mind and mouth betrayed her. She stammered for a moment before managing to blurt out a vaguely benign version of what she really wanted to yell into the phone, "I…I…don't know what I ever could have done to deserve this."

"Oh, no, no. You mustn't think that." Jacqui showed no sign she picked up on Hannah's dismay. "You deserve any and everything we can throw at you."

"I do?"

"Of course you do!" Silly. She didn't say it. But then Jacqui was the kind of person who often said way too much, even on those rare occasions when she had her mouth closed. "Why, we feel so awful about the dreadful way we acted."

"Dreadful," Cydney reiterated. "Just awful."

"We have no choice but to do everything in our power to make it up to you."

"That's not true. You have many, many choices." Missionary work in a tropical island sans telephones. Volunteering to redecorate for the homeless—because they'd be the least traumatized by the effort. Vows of silence. "Many, many choices. And you certainly don't owe me anything."

"Don't we?" Jacqui asked.

"No!"

"We owe you our gratitude, and certainly we owe you our services," the other sister said.

"I couldn't possibly impose."

"Impose? No." Jacqui began and Cydney rushed to finish. "No! We want to do this."

"Do what? Exactly?"

"The Christmas pageant!" they chorused.

Hannah's heart sank.

"Cydney Snowden, volunteer set designer reporting for duty, madam chairperson!"

"Set designer?" Images of flocks of big-tooth sheep sprang to the forefront of Hannah's jumbled thoughts.

"And costume mistress," Jacqui interjected with determined yet perky forcefulness. "Already have some sketches drawn up, and as soon as I find my sewing machine under all the paint tarps and scraps of wood and those three spare ceiling fans in my guest bedroom, we'll be in business for sure."

"Wow." Hannah muttered.

"I knew you'd love it. Didn't I say she'd love it, Cydney?"

"Love it. Jacqui's exact words. We'll talk more about this later."

"Guess I better go start excavating my guest room!"

She thought they said goodbye. She thought she'd replied in kind, but if pressed about it, Hannah wouldn't have gone on record regarding anything about that phone call except to say it left her feeling woozy.

She rubbed her temple as she hung up the phone and wondered aloud, "Maybe Payt *can* prescribe motion sickness pills to keep everyday life from sending my head spinning."

"What?" Sam poked his head around the wall dividing the front room and the kitchen.

"Oh, it's just a joke I made to Aunt Phiz once. How long have you stood there listening in?"

His eyes grew wide. "Uh, n-not long."

"Too bad." She reached out to ruffle his hair. "I hoped maybe you could tell me if I sounded more like a complete fool or just a half-wit."

He laughed, his eyes filled with light when he looked up at her. "You're so funny."

Another compliment.

She put her hand to her chest and met his eager gaze. "I ever tell you that sometimes you just make my day?"

"No, ma'am." He blushed the way boys that age do—across the nose and in the hollow of his freckled cheeks.

If she had thought it wouldn't send him running to get the dog to lick his face clean, she'd have bent down and given the kid a big old smooch on the forehead. "Well, I should tell you, and more often, too."

Grown men who accepted the highest honors given in their most fervent fields of endeavor could not have looked more proud or pleased…or surprised—than this dear, humble, cast-adrift little boy did.

And to think, a year ago at this time she was still telling her sisters she didn't think she could ever relate to any little boy, much less a stranger's child who would need so much. She had almost talked herself out of taking the child at all. But then Payt had promised the life of leisure as a doctor's stay-at-home wife and that she'd have everything she ever dreamed of.

On that point he was so right.

She curved her hand under Sam's chin. "I love you, Sam. You know that, don't you?"

He blinked. His eyes hinted at getting all watery—but only for one fleeting second. Then he squirmed loose, sniffled and scrunched up his nose. "Aw, that love stuff, that's so girly."

He darted down the hall.

"Is not!" she shouted after him. "I happen to know that Payt loves you, too. And Aunt Phiz. Grandpa Moonie loves you and—"

"And Jesus," came back down the darkened hallway that led to his bedroom. "Jesus loves me."

"And Jesus," she said softly. *He gets it.* Sam understood it was not about a baby in a basket and boys in bathrobes. Jesus loved him.

She didn't care if it was all girly—she didn't feel one bit ashamed when a tear rolled down her cheek.

No matter what else this roller coaster of a day held in store for Hannah, she felt certain she could deal with it— even without motion-sickness pills. Nothing could spoil the knowledge that for all the things that went awry, that she didn't seem to have any control over, that she wanted so badly to do and be and always failed, in this one thing, where it mattered most, she had done well.

"Maybe this is a turning point," she murmured to Tessa as she passed the baby working a frozen water-filled ring over tiny swollen gums. "In fact, I'm sure it is. Sam, come keep an eye on…on *your baby sister*…while I go get the mail. Then, if my paycheck from the paper is here, I'm taking the whole family to dinner."

A cheap dinner, to be sure. But feeling as she did, it would seem a feast.

She stepped out the door into the early-fall afternoon filled with hope and expectation.

And the door slammed shut behind her.

16

Hannah Shelnutt Bartlett writes "Nacho Mama's House" from her home just outside of Cincinnati, where she lives with her husband and two young children. Please feel free to send comments and questions to Hannah via the Wileyville Guardian News.

—Bio that runs at the bottom of "Nacho Mama's House" column

Slam!

Hannah nearly jumped out of her skin. She clutched her chest and moaned between her teeth. Too bad she hadn't jumped out of Payt's bathrobe!

A bathrobe. An ill-fitting one over her clothes at that, and in the afternoon. It didn't look good.

She turned to try the door, knowing what she'd find.

"Locked." The action had become second nature to her these days.

Since Aunt Phiz had struck up a friendship with the woman across the street—nice lady, terrible manners—they had adopted a new adage for getting along with their neighbor. *Live and lock up.*

Somehow the woman had gotten the idea that opening a front door and shouting "Knock Knock" was a perfectly acceptable substitute for actually knocking and waiting for her host to ask her in. It didn't help that in Aunt Phiz's absence the woman had decided to take Hannah on as a project. So that left Hannah with two situations—she had to get her mail and she had to not draw the attention of anyone who might want to do her good.

Stealth. That's what this called for. Or, as Aunt Phiz would say, *"Get in, get out, don't get involved."*

She could do this. She only had to negotiate the lawn, cross the sidewalk, hop off the curb, whip open the mailbox, get the goods and go.

Hannah Bartlett, secret agent girl. Except she wasn't a girl and nothing she did anymore seemed the least bit secret. Just the opposite. What with her roles as Snack Mom, church helper, doctor's wife and newspaper columnist, her every move had become fodder for scrutiny.

Just what every person who fears that no one could possibly love them for themselves needs!

She stepped gingerly onto her wide, protected front porch. The October air kissed her cheeks. Just before it whipped her loose auburn waves into a frenzied mass. She cinched the robe tight and Squirrelly Girl's dog toy clunked against her stomach.

She leaned over the white wooden railing to peer down the narrow shady sidewalk. Left. Right. All clear.

"Better get this over with," she whispered. One last scan of the lifeless street and she made her move.

"Hey, neighbor!" The front door of the house across the street thumped shut and a woman in a pale pink jogging suit shot down into her yard, heading straight for Hannah.

"Oh, hi, Lol…" She stopped herself just short of shouting out what Payt called the woman—Lollie, as in Lollie Mulldoon, Wileyville's biggest gossip. The nickname didn't even fit, really. Their bright, energetic neighbor fell more under the heading of aggressively helpful busybody than gossip. Hannah had pointed that out to Payt, who quickly pointed out right back that the only body their Lollie-wannabe continually tried to keep busy was Hannah's—by feeling compelled to give her suggestions for the column.

Grrr. She really hated it when he made a point she couldn't refute with logic or joke her way out of.

But he was right. The woman considered herself Hannah's own Nacho Mama muse, and Hannah felt helpless to do anything about it. She had to see the lady every day, after all.

In fact, she was seeing her right now—only, instead of looking at her, she was staring like a deer in the headlights!

Wave, she commanded her arm.

Smile. Her lips obliged her request.

And, feet? First chance you get—run for it.

"Hi!" For the life of her, she suddenly couldn't recall the woman's real name.

"Nice day." Her pristine athletic shoes hit the street and didn't stop until they'd carried the woman so close, she propped her arm up on Hannah's mailbox.

"Uh-huh." She couldn't stop grinning. Not when she popped open her mailbox, not when she lunged blindly with one hand in to try to retrieve her mail. Not even when she realized that the mailman had wedged something in there so tight that it wasn't going anywhere without a fight.

"How's the writing coming along?"

Hannah tried not to sound panicked as she tugged on a large padded envelope. "Oh, you know, like all work, good days and bad."

"Work? That's so sweet that you call it work."

Hannah froze, elbow-deep in the mailbox. "It is work."

"Oh, I didn't mean that as an insult. I just meant…" She looked away a moment.

Hannah considered propping her foot against the post and using the leverage to extricate the envelope—and herself.

Too late. The woman whipped her head around like one of those defense attorneys in old movies who lulled witnesses into a false sense of security just before they homed in for the kill. "Well, an itty-bitty newspaper column in your hometown newspaper—it's more like writing a letter home than creating literature, isn't it?"

"Well…" Hannah straightened the robe's lapels but didn't argue.

"And I think that's just wonderful!"

She relaxed a bit. "Me, too."

"So cozy and homey." Lollie-lite slipped her hands into the pockets of her jogging jacket. "And so easy."

Yeah, you try it. "I'm sure it seems that way."

"Practically writes itself, doesn't it?" She didn't give Hannah time to answer. Just pulled her hand from her pocket with a flourish and produced a piece of paper. "My sister just told me the cutest story about my nephew. I wrote it down for you. I'm sure she wouldn't mind you sharing it with your readers if you need some inspiration."

"Oh, if I ever get stuck." That was not a lie. She didn't promise anything. In fact she hadn't actually formed a proper sentence.

The neighbor tucked the story into Payt's robe pocket. She must not have made contact with the baby-drool dog toy, because she never flinched, just enthused, "Fabulous."

Backtrack. Confess. She was never, ever going to want to hear, much less use, the precious story about her neighbor's nephew.

"But if you don't need it, don't worry."

Reprieve.

"I have plenty more stories where that one came from."

"Oh. You…uh…you never have read my column, have you?"

"Oh, no, dear. But I know all about those silly women columns. Look at me, I'm so nutty, my family's so nutty." She lifted her hands and waved them around as she spoke.

"I've never called my family nutty." At least not in the newspaper.

"Oh, honey, it's all right. I know you make most of that stuff up. It's good publicity."

"I certainly don't write to draw attention to myself." She tugged her husband's robe closed over her clothes. "I write to communicate real problems of modern motherhood—silliness is not a part of it."

"Hannah, please don't misunderstand. Everyone needs a little silliness from time to time. I'm sure your stories make other mothers your age feel so much better about their lives."

Compared to the mess mine's in? Hannah kept her mouth shut and went in after the envelope. She yanked hard once and out it came, flinging the water and electric bills to the sidewalk along the way.

"If you'll excuse me, I have work to do. Serious work." She shook her hair back, smiled stiffly, then bent to pick up the scattered bills. *Silly work? Silly, indeed! I'd like to show her my work so she could understand that I have things to say, like—*

Squawk! The sound from her pocket virtually echoed through the entire neighborhood.

Hannah went bolt upright. "Dog's squeak toy…in my pocket…forgot."

The lady nodded, slowly, her mouth set in a thin line.

Hannah took one backward step, waved with the envelopes then ran for the house.

She jabbed the doorbell and Sam came to her rescue as she stood there mocking her own pridefulness. "I don't think that's one bit silly. Oh, no, modern motherhood is serious business."

"What?" Sam slid to the floor and picked up his picture-book Bible. He pulled it into his lap even as he poked his leg out to jiggle the laundry basket where Tessa lay worrying the teething ring.

"It's not important, Sam."

He turned to the page about the visitors who followed the star to the stable.

"But this is." She raised the bulky padded packet. "Look, I got paid!"

"Wow, you must make a ton of money!"

She laughed, her humiliation forgotten. "It's not all money, kiddo. They save up the reader mail and send it with any other information they want me to have and my check."

"You get fan mail?"

"Oh, no." Fan mail? Her? The very thought of having fans felt far too self-important. "Reader mail. People write to ask me questions or just to say hello."

"Hello?"

"Remember, my column just runs in my hometown newspaper."

"'Cause you grew up all in the same place and everybody knows you."

Such a simple statement but the wistful longing in his tone went straight through her. Despite the progress they had made, Sam still carried a vulnerability that she readily recognized.

She brushed his cheek with her hand. "Why don't you call one of your soccer buds and see if he wants to go out for pizza with us tonight?"

"Really?"

"Sure. The team directory is on my desk. I was entering some e-mail addresses into my computer. You can use the phone in there."

She hadn't finished the last sentence before he'd shot off toward her tiny home office space.

"Okay, Tessa." She pulled the baby up into her lap. The child nuzzled close and exhaled, and Hannah could feel some of the tension leave her tiny body. She kissed the bright red hair. "If only all the problems you kids will ever have could be solved by pizza and hugs, sweetie. Now, let's you and me read these letters."

She tore into the package and dumped the contents beside her on the couch.

"Check." She held it up. "Hmm, maybe your daddy will pitch in on the pizza."

Tessa grabbed for the computer-generated payment.

Hannah whisked it away, sending a note sailing into her lap. Another reminder from her editor that she really should set up a Nacho Mama Web page.

"Yeah right. Open myself up to a whole World Wide Web of people happy to point out my failings? No thank you."

She stifled a shiver and set the note on the coffee table, then fixed her attention on the envelopes in the pile.

Five. Not bad. Her first week she'd gotten ten, the record. But some of those were e-mails the paper had kindly printed out for her. Four were old friends catching up. One had been a scolding from her seventh-grade English teacher for playing fast and loose with good old-fashioned grammar. After that it had fallen off to two or three a week, mostly kind comments on this or that, the occasional correction and questions that ranged from wanting information on adopting an ex-racing greyhound like Squirrelly Girl to requests to know "Where do you get those really big cans of cheese?"

Reader mail day was often the highlight of Hannah's week. She snuggled down deeper into the cozy cushions of the still-new couch and opened the first letter and then the next and the next. Two notes of encouragement and a high school student doing a project who wondered if Hannah might answer some questions on how she got started.

"I don't think her teacher will like my answer to that much, will she, Tessa? How did you get started in journalism? Answer—against my will." Hannah tucked the pages back inside the proper envelopes and set them aside to answer later.

"This one looks official." She held up the only legal-size envelope in the bunch and tried to remember where she had seen the logo before.

"'The Faith-Filled Home,'" she read from the letterhead inside. "Oh, yeah. I've seen their magazine in the church office."

A subscription sales pitch probably. She read on. "Not that I have time to read for pleasure these—"

Not an offer to read, an offer to *write*. "We have read the columns in your local paper with interest, and would be open to future submissions of new material for possible use in our magazine."

Hannah showed the paper to her daughter, careful to keep it just out of reach of those sticky fingers. "My editor at the paper is a friend of the editor of the magazine and sent some of my stuff over, and looks like they are 'open' to me submitting to them. I wonder what that means in editor-ese?"

Tessa rolled off Hannah's lap and onto the couch, crawled to the back and started to pull herself up.

"Open? As in 'We get so much of this stuff, another few won't matter'? Or 'open,' as in 'I saw something of worth in this stuff and wouldn't mind seeing what more you can do'?"

The baby bounced at the knees a few times, clutching the back of the couch, like a rock climber about to make her ascent.

"The second. Definitely the second. I mean, if I have to choose…I choose the second option. Your daddy says for me to listen to the way I talk about myself, and he's right. I am saying here and now that I can do this. I can produce something worthy of national publication."

Her heart rate did a dance. Her throat went dry. "Listen to me! Did you hear that? I actually admitted I could do this."

If…

Her eye fell on the single, pulse-stopping word on the page in her hand.

She drew a deep breath and made herself go silently over the proviso. "Needs polish…writing lacks focus… humor not enough to interest our readers…used as teaching tool…draw some pertinent spiritual lessons from your essays on daily life for our readers."

Tessa sank slowly to sit on the couch. She grabbed the teething ring from Hannah's lap and her mouth worked furiously on it for a few seconds before she batted the thing away.

Hannah held her breath, willing the child not to yowl out her frustration. "I won't if you won't."

Tessa stretched, poked one tiny fist into the air, found a comfy position and relaxed into a chubby little ball in the crevice of couch cushions.

Hannah could not let go of her discomfort so easily. Probably, she reasoned, because it sprang from the deep, dark truth she knew about herself.

As a writer, she stank.

Or was that *stunk?* See? She didn't even know the right word for sure.

The paper crackled in her hand.

"Still." She chewed her lower lip. If she wanted to become a better writer, she needed experience and guidance.

If she did accept the offer to try her hand at freelancing for a national magazine, she'd get both.

"Imagine that, sweetie." She kissed her baby's forehead. "Mommy has a chance to not stink. Do you suppose that's possible?"

She kissed the child again, took a tiny sniff to make sure Tessa could make that same bold "not stinking" claim, then paper-clipped the offer to her check so she could consider it in depth later.

"Okay, one last reader letter, then I have to get with it. I still have to try to get a hold of your daddy and make plans for pizza tonight."

She lifted the final envelope. It was pale blue and squarish, like it might contain one of those artsy cards with a postage-stamp-size black-and-white photo in the center. The kind of thing someone would go to a card shop and comb through the displays to find just the right one.

Hannah smiled at the thought of anyone going to such trouble for her. In fact, she still marveled that people took the time and effort to write her at all. She found it sweet and humbling and a little bit exhilarating all at once.

Letters—in a day and age when people just didn't take the time and trouble. She flipped the blue envelope over to see if she recognized the name on the return address, but there was none.

"Hmm." She slid her finger under the flap. "Ouch!"

Instinctively she shook her hand until the tiny sting subsided. She glanced at the inside of her knuckle, then heavenward with a smile. "Is this is your way of making sure I stay humble while reading fan mail, Lord?"

She laughed, not because she found any great wit in herself but because she felt a great contentment. Her children were healthy. Her son was making important strides in his spiritual growth. By her work and talent she had brought in enough money to provide her family with a special treat, and somebody thought she had the potential to be a decent writer.

She ripped open the blue flap and pulled free the delicate floral-covered notecard. "Let's see what this nice, faithful reader has to say, shall we, Tessa?"

"*Dear Mrs. Bartellet,*" it began.

"Oops, misspelled my name. Guess she's not that faithful of a reader after all."

Hannah squinted at the cramped handwriting scaled down to fill every centimeter of white space on the inside of the card and her breathing went still.

17

Subject: Venting and reinventing
To: ItsmeSadie, WeednReap
Dear Sadie and April,
If I add I'm praying for you at the end of a response to criticism does that make it all right to be snarky? For example:

Dear Reader,

Thank you for your letter, and for taking the time from your obviously busy schedule of kicking puppies and shoving little old ladies into oncoming traffic, to share with me the many reasons why you think I am as ill suited to be a foster mom as I am unfit to be a writer. You present so many thought-provoking opinions. For instance, the thoughts they provoked in me were: You don't know me or my family or what you are talking about when you presume to pass judgment on us. You are probably just a big miserable meanie with way too much time on your hands because you don't have any friends or family of your own. Oh, and your penmanship is the pits. God Bless.

Or:

Dear Reader,

I noted from the misspelling of my name on the card that you were looking for a Mrs. Bartellet. As my last name is Bartlett I can understand the confusion and why your concerned letter was mistakenly forwarded to me. Am returning it with best regards and faith that you will in time find the object of your dissatisfaction.

Or:

Dear Reader,

Thank you for your frank and forceful letter wherein you called my work intellectual garbage and referred to me as a glib-talking airhead who has only made one valid point in her entire writing career—that her readers should all be praying for the welfare of her children.

As I sit here rereading your thoughts again and again, I cannot escape the reality. It's true. All true. You have given voice to the suspicions I have long harbored but would never let myself fully embrace. I am no writer. I came to the craft much as I did foster parenting—by default. I once foolishly thought that maybe God had guided me into these things for His higher reasons.

I wonder if I had convinced myself of that because I so longed to hope, just a little, that I was worthy. That someone wanted me. But now…

Of course I'll only send these to you and thank you and thank the Lord for your understanding and prayers.
Love,
Hannah

"You're not eating your pizza." Payt pushed the stark white plate toward her. "Your idea, you know, to come here and celebrate your big payday."

"Celebrate?" She lifted the crust and let it drop. "I don't feel like celebrating anything anymore."

"Over a letter? One lousy, almost unreadable letter?"

"*I* could read it." Every word.

He reached across the table to help himself to her slice. "Yeah, well, I wish you hadn't."

"Me, too." She spoke in a small voice. It fit. She felt small. Insignificant.

"Ask 'em. Ask 'em." The boys returned from the game room. The friend Sam had asked along for pizza nudged him in the shoulder. "Go on, ask."

Payt leaned close to Sam. "I think your friend…Stilton?"

"Hunter," Hannah hurried to correct, giving the boys a what-can-you-do?-the-man-*never*-listens eye roll for good measure. "I can't believe you got that wrong."

She couldn't. Not after she had rattled on and on gushing her gratitude that Sam had picked Hunter over Stilton. About how she felt crummy enough this evening without the offspring of the world's greatest mom sitting at the table telling her his mom made pizza at home, without cheese on account of his lactose intolerance.

"Bet she brews her own root beer, too," Hannah muttered.

"Hmm?" Payt's brow crimped downward.

"Nothing. I was just…" Acting petty. Normal. Small and petty. "It was nothing. I think Hunter wants to ask us something."

Sam held his hands up in the universal language of kids that says "Don't ask me why" as he said, "He wants to hear your talk."

"My talk?" Payt frowned, a big phony, perplexedlike frown. He really hammed it up. Scratching his head and pulling on his ear like he couldn't believe what he'd heard. "Would you like to attend a lecture on pediatric endocrinology, young man?"

The dark-haired child about to explode into a shower of giggles at the end of the table let out a long, loud "No-o-o-o."

"Well, maybe I misunderstood you then. You say you want to hear my sock?" He raised his leg and tugged at the red socks he wore to work to amuse the children. "People have told me they were loud, but I don't think you can actually hear them."

"No-o-o-o," Hunter managed to eke out between giggles.

Giggles. Not little, sweet, endearing ones, either. But great trying-to-hold-it-back eight-year-old-boy gulping giggles, like when one accuses the other of unleashing…an obnoxious odor.

Sam joined in.

Payt shook his head.

Hannah clued him in. "He wants to hear our accents."

"Accent?" Only Payt pronounced it more like *aix-ssent*. He proceeded to lay on the hokum extra thick, proclaiming, "We ain't got no accent. Y'all the ones got the accents."

"Nuh-uh. You're the one with the accent." Hunter pointed at Payt while the boy shifted from foot to foot. "You and Mrs. Bartlett. She says Nacho Mama's house when she means not your mama's house!"

"Oh, dear! Do you do that?" Payt put on regal British airs this time. "Shocking!"

"Keep making fun of me and I'll show you shocking, Bartlett. Knock those red socks right off your feet."

He leaned in close to her, close enough that she could feel his breath when he whispered, "You always knock my socks off, Nacho Mama."

"Come on, Hunter. It's going to get mushy around here." Sam bumped his friend's arm in passing as he turned toward the game room a few feet away. "Let's go back and watch those guys play air hockey."

Hunter started to go along, stopped, then whipped his head around and wrinkled his nose. "Hey, how come you talk normal, Sam, and your parents don't?"

Sam's cheeks blanched. He fixed his gaze on the game room across the way. "They're not my—"

"Because we're just a couple of great big old hicks." Payt pretended to pick his teeth with the straw as he looped his arm around his foster son's waist and said, "And Sam here is one of them citified sophisticates."

"Your dad is funny." Hunter punched Sam in the arm. "Race ya."

And just that fast they rushed off to watch some older boys play air hockey. At the edge of the wide arch that separated the game room from the main dining room, Sam stopped.

Hannah laid her hand on her husband's forearm and directed his attention with a flick of her head.

Gratitude. Admiration. Anxiety and hope. With a single brief glance, Sam summed up it all up.

"You did good," Hannah whispered in her husband's ear.

"Yeah, who'd a thunk a slob of a kiddie doctor might know his way around talking to a couple eight-year olds?"

"It's more than that and you know it. You're a natural with kids, Payt."

"Thanks."

She gazed after the boys a moment before fixing her attention on Tessa. On a Tessa with pudding smeared all over her face.

Great. She had brought dry cereal for the child to snack on. Nice, safe, clean dry cereal. In a little yellow tub made just for carting it around.

And Payt had taken one look at the salad bar, sized up what an eight-month-old baby could have and plunked down enough for a kiddie meal. And Tessa had loved it.

Obviously.

Hannah grabbed up a cloth napkin and started to spit and dab on the baby's cheeks. "You don't have to stop and think through every little thing to decide what's the right thing to say or do."

"Neither do you, Hannah, if you'd just relax a little and trust yourself." He lifted another slice of pizza from the box and held it out toward her. "And, please, eat something."

The aroma of freshly baked dough and spicy sauce assaulted her senses. She squeezed her eyes shut. "It's not that easy."

"Sure it is. Just open your mouth, bite down and chew."

"Hey, just because Hunter thinks you're funny, don't go planning your comedy tour, not with that kind of material." She pushed the slice in his hand away.

"Hannah, we have all this pizza."

"I can't eat any. Not now."

"Then quit."

"What?"

"Quit."

"Eating?"

"No." He dropped the slice of pizza back onto the plate with a dead *thud.* "Quit writing the column."

"What?" Hannah experienced her own thud—like her heart falling into her stomach. Her husband wanted her to quit writing. He had to be kidding. Of course, the big comedian. She folded her arms. "Are you saying that to try to get me riled, or because you honestly think I should quit?"

"Whichever makes you happy."

She smirked. "*Happy* happy or happy enough to wolf down some pizza?"

"Both." He kissed her once lightly.

She laid her hand along his cheek as he pulled away. "You make me happy, Bartlett."

"Good, because it's a sure thing writing this column doesn't." He motioned to the waitress to bring them a box for the leftover pizza.

"Wait a minute, you're the one who told me to do the column. You told me to follow my dream and write."

"And you've done it." He opened the large white cardboard box on the table and began flopping slices covered in cheese and pepperoni into it. "No one can take that away from you. But if you don't find it rewarding, you don't have to keep at it."

"I never said I didn't find writing rewarding." *Had she?* She did a quick survey of their conversations on the topic.

Frustrating. Yes, she'd said that.

Exhilarating. On a good day. For those few hours after she'd turned in her last piece (before she started worrying about how lousy it was). And when she came up with the inspiration for a new column. Very exhilarating. She must have told him that.

And what else?

Daunting. Uh-huh, daunting. She'd definitely called it daunting at some point.

But *unrewarding?* Hmm. No, she couldn't recall having used that particular description for her work.

She whirled around in her seat and angled her chin up at him. "I got an offer to write for a national publication, you know. That's a pretty nice reward."

He closed the box lid and popped the tabs in place to secure it. "Hannah, you make me crazy."

"Yeah?"

"Yeah." He slipped his fingers down the lock of auburn hair that brushed her chin. "In a good way. Yeah."

"Do you…" She picked up the to-go box, stood and waved the boys over to the table. With her back to her hubby—because she wanted to make sure the boys didn't dawdle, not because she couldn't bear to look him in the eye—she asked quietly, "Do you think I'm a rotten writer?"

"No."

"Then why—" She spun around.

Thwack.

The box knocked him in the back of the head.

"I am so sorry. I didn't mean to… Are you okay?" She dropped the box onto the table and began stroking the soft, closely cropped hair, not sure if she was searching for blood or pizza sauce.

"I'm fine." He batted her hand away.

"Good." She gave his head the tiniest of pushes and said, "Then why did you tell me to quit writing?"

"You know that old joke?"

She folded her arms. "So now I'm an old joke?"

"No." He held his hand up. "Hear me out."

"Okay." At least he hadn't asked her to listen to herself, for which she was extremely grateful, because she suspected she sounded like a lunatic.

"There's that old joke. Man goes to his doctor and says, 'Doc, it hurts when I do this.'" He moved his arm stiffly back and forth. His earnest eyes held her gaze. "So the doctor tells him…"

Hannah crooked her own arm and let it swing. "'Don't do that.'"

"One of the first things we learned in medical school." He caught her hand midsway and kissed her knuckles one by one. "That."

Kiss.

"And…"

Kiss.

"That you have to eat."

Kiss.

"To stay alive."

Kiss and turning her hand over, *kiss* again.

"I'll warm some of this up later." She tapped the box.

"Good. You have to keep your strength up for our trip."

"Our trip." She shut her eyes and could almost feel the warmth on her face. Maybe the future of her writing career looked bleak, but her marriage had definitely taken a turn toward the sunny side. She smiled and whispered, "Miami."

"You deserve the break." He stood, too, placing his hand on her back.

Hannah savored the warmth of his touch as she would a long, sweet embrace.

Tessa kicked.

The boys reached the table, finally. After they had stopped along the way to check for a penny on the floor and went back to start at the same spot so they could determine once and for all who could hop on one foot the longest between the game room and the table.

Payt bent and released the tray on the high chair enough to get Tessa out. He lifted her up.

She kicked hard, sending droplets of pudding from her shoes plopping on Payt's pants and Hannah's arm.

"And after we get back from our trip, maybe you won't want to keep up with the column anyway." He handed the baby to her.

"Why?" For a half a second she considered carrying her chocolate-covered baby to the car at an arm's length. Then Tessa laughed and Hannah pulled her close, drawing in the smell of oat cereal and pudding. "After a break most people are ready to get back to their work with a whole new attitude."

"Sure, but after you get back from this break, maybe you'll be too busy."

"Haven't you heard? Jacqui and Cydney are pitching in on the pageant. That should lighten my load. Especially after they blow up the set and sew the costumes into one big circus tent for our performance."

"Don't worry about the pageant. It'll go great." He nabbed the box and directed the boys to lead the way out. "Think beyond the pageant to the big picture."

"Oh, I don't think we should try to make the pageant

into a big picture. Maybe one of those small, independent films that doesn't make any money but gets the rave reviews."

"Stop kidding, Hannah." He stepped back to hold the door for everyone to go through ahead of him. "I'm talking about our life. Our family."

"I'll stop kidding if you'll stop sounding so scary serious."

"Serious, yes, but not scary."

An unexpected autumn rain must have blown through while they were eating and had drenched the parking lot. They walked together through the scent of damp pavement and rain-filtered air.

"I'm listening." Hannah wrestled Tessa into the car seat while the boys scrambled into the back bench of the minivan and buckled up.

"Hannah, it's just that we're not getting any younger."

"Hey, you promised no scary stuff." She sat down and snapped her own seat belt into place.

Payt climbed into the driver's seat. He checked the mirror, then nudged Hannah. With a nod of his head he urged her to look into the mirror to catch Hunter trying to fasten a safety belt around the pizza box while Sam lectured Tessa on the importance of always wearing a safety belt.

She smiled at her husband. "Too cute, huh?"

"Just cute enough," he said. "Give you any ideas?"

"No, but it should give you one—buckle up, Bartlett." She jerked her thumb toward his shoulder harness. "And stop trying to distract me from the fact that you just said we're a couple of old coots."

"We? Did I say *we?*"

"Do they make safety belts for mouths, because I know someone who might like to try one." She gave him a good-humored glare. "You were saying?"

"I was saying that aging isn't scary, sweetheart."

"Sure, not for you. You're a gorgeous physician."

"What's that got to do with anything?"

"Don't even pretend with me that you don't know that aging is easier on attractive men in positions of wealth and/or power."

"What power do I have? Because I sure don't have wealth."

"You have me and the kids—we're priceless."

"I'll remember that next time I'm paying bills." He gave her a grin and a wink.

"Anyway, you know what I'm saying. Look at Dr. Briggs. He's a prime example of a man that knows he doesn't have to be young or particularly charming to still get his way in life."

"That wasn't very nice."

"Payt, I'm just saying—"

"I'd have thought you of all people would know better than to rush to judgment about another human being."

"Right." She folded her hands in her lap and focused on the passing landscape of rain-washed buildings.

"Sorry, I…I shouldn't have jumped on you. I only wanted to say that aging isn't inherently frightening. But that I do find the thought of getting older and looking back with regrets scary. To realize that I missed out on things I shouldn't have because of some unfounded hesitation or distraction because I was too busy with things that didn't matter in the long run—that's scary."

"You draw a very compelling big picture there, Payt." She tucked her hair back and waited while the windshield wipers thrashed back and forth a few times before adding, "Maybe a little too big. Kind of like those photos that take a simple object and magnify it until you can't tell if you're seeing the surface of Mars or a close-up of an orange peel."

"Let me scale it down for you. Scaling down, scaling back—it's all part of the same argument anyway."

Scale down. Scale back. Just hearing the words made her feel better. "Scaling down—you wouldn't happen to be referring to your suggestions that I quit the column?"

"Hannah, sometimes you have to pick and choose."

"And you've suggested that after the break I'll be too busy for everything I've been doing."

"Sometimes less is more."

"And tossed in a little cowboy philosophy about not looking back with regrets."

"Time comes to set your priorities, Hannah."

"Why do I have the feeling it's not my priorities you're big-picturing here?"

"Mine, yours, ours—is there really that much difference?"

"Spit it out, Bartlett. What have you got in mind for us to pick and choose, more or less?"

He didn't say a word, just looked up at the rearview mirror and stared at the kids all cozy and safe in the back seat.

And Hannah knew exactly what he meant.

"Oh, no. You have got to be kidding."

18

Subject: Countdown to Miami
To: ItsmeSadie, WeednReap
Hey, y'all. I should be working on my column, but instead I'm counting down:

  10—number of enormous bags of unpopped popcorn from the warehouse club sitting in my living room

  9—number of times I've told Payt I cannot come in and clean the office one more time before we leave for Florida

  8—rewrites done on this week's column, due in

  7—hours

  6—hours until we leave for the airport

  5—e-mails with attachments, including costume and set design ideas marked "urgent," sent by the DIY sisters this morning

4—moms who volunteered to help with the class fund-raising project

3—bags packed (and repacked) waiting by the door

2—plane tickets tucked neatly in a zippered compartment in my purse

1—last straw standing between me and…

"Here, let's do the baby ones first." Lauren Faison held up the fabric shell of a soon-to-be-stuffed beanbag frog. "Babies should be easy, don't you think?"

"Me? I think babies are…" She blinked in the direction of Tessa's nursery. The child had kept her up most of the night. Not that she minded since anticipation kept her from sleeping anyway. But this morning when the child's fussiness hadn't abated, Hannah didn't feel quite so accepting. She rubbed her fingers over her tight scalp. "Believe me, babies are anything but easy."

"Don't worry. Your aunt has everything under control."

Poor Aunt Phiz. Only back in town an hour, and already pressed into service walking Tessa through the neighborhood so Hannah and Lauren could try to make some progress on their school fund-raising project.

She lifted up the empty beanbag frog she was supposed to turn right side out. "So, absolutely no way we could just throw together a bake sale?"

"None." Lauren grabbed her frog by the feet, gave it a flap and the fabric popped. A little shake. A prod with a pencil for the arms and legs and done. A bullfrog-shaped bag ready for stuffing.

"Why not?" Hannah tugged this way and that. A foot here, and arm there. A twist. A shout. And…the poor thing looked like one right-side-out plaid frog swallowing one of its inside-out brethren. "Is the school worried about kids with allergies? We could label everything clearly to get around that."

Lauren dropped her third expertly turned frog onto a stack. "Hannah, I didn't want to admit this, but you leave me no choice."

Hannah ditched her feetfirst frog behind her back. "What?"

Lauren batted her gorgeous lashes, shifted her size-six hips then tucked a strand of highlighted golden hair behind her ear. Her diamond stud earring flashed. She cleared her throat. "I am the one who put the kibosh on having a bake sale as a fund-raiser."

"Kibosh?" Hannah picked a wayward thread from the tip of her tongue.

"Nixed. Eighty-sixed. No deal."

"I know what it means, but I don't understand why you feel that way."

"Why? Isn't it obvious?"

You don't want to risk me poisoning small children? Listen, Hannah. The woman never said anything like that. Not every statement is a judgment. Get a clear answer before you start assuming the worst.

"I'm sorry, it's not obvious to me. Seems like getting together a few dozen cookies and cupcakes would be a lot easier than this." She dangled her wad-o-frog mess before

Lauren's eyes, dropped it in her lap, then spread her arms to indicate the two dozen forms draped over every surface of her living room.

"Well, yeah, sure. If we could just 'get together' the goods. But a bake sale requires a bit more than that."

"Like what?"

"Baking, for starters."

Hannah nodded, chuckling. "One would think."

"And mixing and pouring."

"Yep. With you so far."

"And preheating and cooling on racks and, well, I shudder to mention…"

Hannah braced herself. If something made Lauren Faison quake, it might likely send Hannah into convulsions.

"Frosting." Lauren winced.

Convulsions? No. But she did suddenly have the urge to bang her head on the floor in humiliation. "I see."

"Oh, don't take it personally, Hannah. It's a good idea but it's just—"

Don't take it personally? How could she not? The most together mom in the world, whose son had actually bragged about her homemade goodies, who had literally caught Hannah spreading spackling compound on a children's cake, had just invoked the F-word—frosting!

"Besides, these frogs will make more money, and we can store whatever we don't sell in the garage, unlike most baked goods."

Most baked goods. Not yours, Hannah. Yours would be right at home on a workbench, but the rest of ours…

"I understand."

"I knew you would. Not like you have time to bake right now anyway, not with the big trip just looming."

"Looming. Good word."

"You don't sound enthused."

"Oh, I am. I...am."

"But?"

Hannah picked up another limp froggy and skimmed her fingers along the quarter-inch seam. "Stilton's your only child, isn't he?"

"Oh, I get it." Lauren slipped orange plaid fabric over itself and deposited another finished frog body onto her growing pile. "Worried about leaving the kids behind, right?"

"No." Hannah's second attempt fell into her lap half-done. "Worried about bringing another one home with us."

"Oh, Hannah! Another baby? That's terrific. Are you?"

"No. Not yet." She sighed. "But Payt thinks it's time we started, um, a family expansion project."

"And perhaps you don't feel ready?"

Hannah could only nod.

"Hmm." Lauren kept at her work. "How old is Tessa?"

"Right at eight months, but the thing is, it took me almost two years to get pregnant with her. And as my darling husband pointed out at the pizza parlor last night—I'm not getting any younger."

Work stopped. Lauren leaned in, placing her chin in one manicured hand, to study Hannah with her eyes narrowed. "Cheese or pepperoni?"

"Huh?"

"Just wondering which kind of pizza you dumped in his lap for that remark."

Hannah laughed. "Neither. I just sat there, stunned."

"By the age thing or the baby thing?"

"The baby. Definitely the baby."

"Don't you want another one?"

Didn't she? Who wouldn't want another baby?

Maybe a woman who daily questioned her ability to nurture and raise her current baby.

"I don't know. Maybe. Maybe not. I think maybe our family feels complete already with Sam and Tessa. But what if Sam's biological father takes him away? And if Payt wants another child…"

"You really are up in the air about this baby issue, aren't you?"

"Up in the air. Down in the dumps. No wonder I'm afraid that if I don't find some equilibrium soon, time may leave me high and dry."

"Then don't let it. And don't be afraid, Hannah—leave it with the Lord and pray, and you'll find your answers."

"Thanks, Lauren." She smiled, unconvinced the other woman truly understood her dilemma.

They sat there in silence for a moment, focused on the project.

Hannah couldn't help but steal a peek at the other woman's long, elegant fingers at work, though. Lauren's rings glittered but never once snagged. She used her long, lovely nails as tools for poking seams into points, but the polish never chipped. How could someone like that comprehend how tender Hannah found the topic of adding to her family? If Lauren Faison wanted another baby, she'd do it without hesitation or mussing her hairdo.

If she wanted another child. But Lauren didn't have another child. That meant she had to have faced the questions Hannah now faced and somehow come to a decision. A decision? Being Lauren, she had most likely arrived at the ideal conclusion.

Hannah had to hear it. She wet her lips and held her project in both hands in her lap. "Lauren, did you…*do* you ever think about having another child?"

"Me? No! Time has already run out on that for me."

"Yeah, right."

"Well, I was thirty-six when I had Stilton."

"Thirty-six? No way. That would make you…"

"Don't start counting on your fingers, if you don't mind. Suffice it to say the baby train has left the station for me, and that's okay."

"You're at peace with that?"

"Uh-huh. Stilton's dad is sixteen years older than me, you know."

Hannah had heard as much before she even met Lauren, but she never delved.

"And I was no sweet young thing when we met. In fact, I'd given up on finding a good, decent, marriage-minded man of faith completely, and thrown myself into my own real-estate business when Elliot came in to sell his house.

He'd been widowed for two years, and the youngest child had gone off to college. He wanted to downsize."

"So you sold his house?"

"Actually, I married him and moved into it." Lauren laughed. "I won't pretend I didn't have plans to fill it up with children then. But then Stilton was born with a heart defect."

Hannah gasped. "I didn't know."

"Small thing." She held her thumb and forefinger close together to illustrate. "Huge scare. But it really taught us the blessing of leaving things in God's hands."

"What a story. So you chose not to have more kids because of Stilton's health?"

"Hannah, what part of leaving it in God's hands didn't you get?" Lauren patted her hand. "It just didn't happen and that's that. All things turn out for the good for those who love the Lord, and all."

Then your life isn't one-hundred-percent perfection every minute of every day? You've had disappointments and things to overcome, too? She held her tongue, even though it almost killed her not to blurt out her latest revelation for confirmation.

"Anyway, my husband has three grown children. And two of them even have children, so if I need a baby fix I have the ultimate luxury of spoiling someone I can give back."

"You're like a grandmother?"

"Pretty much, yeah."

"I can't believe it. You look so…" Rested. Pulled together. "Vivacious."

"Ooooh, great word. You must be a writer."

"Some would argue otherwise." She could visualize the blue square envelope leaning against her computer monitor even now. "But back to you, how do you do it? How do you do all the things you do for Stilton and look so fresh?"

"You know that saying—'it takes a village to raise a child'?"

"Yes."

"Well, there ought to be a new one—it takes a major metropolitan area to maintain a middle-aged lady."

They shared a laugh.

"The main thing—" Lauren took the mangled shell of a beanbag from Hannah's hands and righted it without any real effort "—you have to make time for yourself. The things you need to be a good wife and mother and friend don't come measured out in hours and minutes. They come from the well of your spirit. If you let that go dry by always giving and never tending to yourself, you have nothing left to give."

"Sounds so easy when you say it. And so wonderful."

"It sounds like a goofy watercolor-painted greeting card left over from the seventies."

"Yeah, but that doesn't make it any less true."

"Now you're getting it. So, tell me right now, what are you doing to care for your physical, mental and spiritual needs?"

"Physical? Chase kids." She hadn't stuck with an exercise program or a diet or even kept a hair appointment since they'd moved to Ohio.

"Mental?" Lauren asked.

"Does figuring out the amount of unpopped popcorn we needed to stuff two dozen frogs count?"

"You write," Lauren reminded her.

"That may be more of a mental illness than a mental endeavor."

Lauren raised her knees and folded her tanned, sculpted arms on top of them. "You certainly expend a great deal of mental energy putting yourself down. But that doesn't count, either. What about your spiritual life?"

"Since I took over the nursery department, I haven't attended one grown-up Sunday service."

"Prayer life?"

"Prayer lite is more like it."

"Time in the Word?"

"Lesson plans, reading to Sam."

"Oh, Hannah…"

"I know. I'm a wreck, aren't I?"

"Oh, we're all wrecks—some of us just take time to hammer the dents out."

She smiled and tried to think of a way to thank Lauren for the advice and humor, but the phone cut her off.

"Excuse me."

"Bartlett Frog Flippers, Miami North Pad."

"Um…Hannah?"

"Oh, no. Don't even ask."

"I wasn't."

"I do not have the time or the inclination to rush over to your office and scour the bathroom."

"I know, but…"

"I mean, come on, Bartlett. It's bad enough that you asked me to do it twice a week already after days of caring for the kids, work and whatever volunteer jobs I've spent my day up to my nose in."

"I know, but…"

"But to keep asking me today is unfair, especially with our trip just a few hours away."

"I know, but…"

"Which, by the way, is the only reason I am not letting out a primal scream of frustration and slamming this phone down in your ear—the knowledge that in a few short hours you, my most darling husband, will be whisking me away for the romantic escape of a lifetime."

Silence met her ramblings.

Not good.

"Payt, honey?" Her pulse raced, she took a shallow breath. "This is the part where you say 'I know but…'"

"Listen, Hannah."

"No." For months now the man had demanded she listen—but to herself, not to him. Listening to him right now, she decided on the spot, could not lead to anything good.

"There's been a little dustup at work."

"That had better not be a weak cleaning joke."

"I wish."

Her heart thudded hard in her ears. "Why?"

"Let's just say the animals in our little metaphorical zoo here started eating each other alive."

"So?" She forced a very unconvincing laugh. "What's a few teeth marks between friends?"

"Hannah, you're not making this easier."

"Okay, how about I make it real easy? Mindless office bickering is not your problem, Bartlett. Your biggest problem today is whether you can pick me up and carry me over the threshold for the start of our second honeymoon."

"I don't think so, Hannah."

She didn't want to ask, but ask or not, the man would eventually have to tell her. "We're not going, are we?"

"We're going."

She fell back against the wall and exhaled.

"Just not right now."

"What?"

"We will go, Hannah. But not today."

What could she say? She'd looked forward to this trip for so long. She needed this getaway so badly. "Payt, please, don't do this. Can't you find a way to—"

"Kaye quit."

And that was that. No way could Dr. Briggs keep the office going with Payt *and* his nurse practitioner gone.

"No trip. No Miami. No flying away from it all."

"Not for good, just for now."

"B-but I had my heart set on *now.* I was counting on now."

"And I am counting on you."

Counting on her. The man she loved was counting on her. Her stomach clenched. He couldn't have used a more deeply connected or dreaded phrase unless he'd added something about all the sick little children and their harried, desperate parents counting on her, too.

"When I bought the ticket, I made sure the travel agent understood this kind of thing might happen," he went on.

"That Kaye might up and quit without warning hours before our flight?"

"That as a doctor I might have to cancel at the eleventh hour. It will cost a little more, but we can change our travel plans."

"Don't even start with me about the cost, just tell me what you want me to do."

"Just go down to the travel agent—you need to go there to handle it all in person so there are no slipups with the flight or the hotel reservations. Can you do that?"

"I can."

"Will you?"

"What choice do I have?"

"Great. I gotta run."

She gripped the receiver, willing herself to place it gently back in its cradle.

You have to make time for yourself. The things you need to be a good wife and mother and friend don't come measured out in hours and minutes. They come from the well of your spirit. If you let that go dry by always giving and never tending to yourself, you have nothing left to give.

Sappy seventies sentiment or not, Hannah found herself gravitating to Lauren's words of wisdom and wondering…

Hannah walked slowly into the living room.

"One of our wayward class moms calling to get directions?" Lauren asked.

"Hardly."

"Too bad, because I have to run."

Startled from her musing, Hannah blinked and discovered her eyes damp with the threat of tears. "You, too?"

"Don't peg me for a deserter just yet. Stilton has a piano lesson, then Tae Kwon Do. In fact, he has a class or homework or we have church or something almost every day of the week."

"Wow."

"Tell me about it. I haven't had a full afternoon free since that kid had his first Tumble Tots class at three."

"Six years?"

"And only nine more to go. Sometimes I think we overschedule him, but then I don't know what we'd cut out and still feel we'd given him every advantage to get into a top-rated college."

"College?" She was supposed to be laying the groundwork for college already?

"But so I won't leave you in the lurch." She waggled one stuffed finished frog in the air by the feet to keep popcorn from spilling out. "Suppose we divvy up the duties?"

"I…" Hannah looked around in a daze, not sure how she felt, what she thought or what she needed to do. "I don't have anything big enough to put half the popcorn in."

"That's easy—you put it into the frogs."

"You've lost me."

"We've got them all turned and ready, you pour the popcorn in, then set them open, seam-up, in a box for me to finish. You stuff, I stitch." She made a broad sewing motion, her pinched thumb and forefinger holding an imaginary needle.

"Right. That's probably for the best, anyway. The way I feel right now, I really shouldn't be handling sharp objects."

"You going to be okay?"

"I think I can manage to fill up a few frogs." Why not? She had all the time in the world, now.

"Okay, just have your aunt bring them to school when she picks up Sam this afternoon, okay?"

"Sure." She didn't have the energy to explain that she'd be available to do the car pool today after all.

"And have a great trip."

"Actually, I—"

R-r-r-r-ring!

First thing tomorrow she was going to discontinue phone service. And e-mail. And her cell phone. And disable her doorbell and…

And it would have been so much more practical to just run away from it all.

R-r-r-r-ring!

"I'll let myself out." Lauren already had the front door open wide.

For a split second Hannah thought of making a break for it. Just go. Get out. Fly away. But just as quickly the door fell shut and the phone demanded her attention again.

R-r-r-r-

"Bartlett Frog Farm, where dreams go to croak."

"Hannah?"

"Payt?" She swallowed hard. Her pulse did a little jig. "It was all a big joke, right? A prank? Something to shake the cobwebs off the old wife before the vacation starts?"

"Sorry, no."

"Oh. What do you need, then?" Too bad he never stopped and asked her what she needed anymore. No one did. Just what they needed from her.

"Well, since your aunt is here to take care of the kids. And since you've got to get out of the house to deal with the travel agent, I had a thought."

Wait a minute. He talked like a man with a plan. A whole new plan. A plan to make up for the lousy change of plans he'd dropped on her earlier. "Yes?"

"Well, there's no reason now why you can't pop in and clean the office tonight after all."

"And there it is, ladies and gents."

"What? Hannah, what are you talking about?"

It.

The line.

The final push.

The point of no return.

The last straw.

Hannah clucked her tongue. She'd made up her mind just that fast, and she saw no purpose in launching into any further explanation. She just told her husband not to expect her in the office today, and if he had any questions, well, he'd get his answers when he got home.

She hung up the phone and picked up a pen.

19

Subject: Change of plans
To: DocPayt
Dear Payt,
I won't be taking the tickets back to the travel agent.
   Call you from Miami.
Love,
Hannah

"What was I thinking?" she asked the lady crowding the armrest and most of the so-called legroom somewhere over Tennessee.

"I really shouldn't do this," she said to the too-polite-to-tell-her-it-wasn't-his-problem man behind the ticket counter when she changed planes in Atlanta.

"The reservation may be for five days, but I'll have to

go back before that, I think," she warned the effervescent clerk in the relaxed elegance of the marble lobby of the five-star hotel in Miami.

In the room, she took in the calming atmosphere, the fresh smell, the bed made by somebody else and towels that would appear clean and fluffed daily without her having to lift a laundry basket. She threw open the curtains to enjoy the endless starlit sky and view of dazzling light reflected through the blue of the pool six stories down. That's when she turned to the bellman, pressed a generous tip into his hand and whispered, "Tell housekeeping to keep the supply of towels coming. I'm going to be here a while."

She had done it.

Her.

The woman who had spun her wheels in a tidy rut for her whole lifetime hoping somehow to please others had finally taken a stand and taken flight.

And to a place where it was far too warm to think about Christmas pageants.

A place sans an office and therefore devoid of office politics—and messy break rooms that needed her attention.

A little corner of the world where no one had ever heard of the DIY-Namic Duo.

And where, if anyone wanted a snack, they called room service.

"Peace," she murmured, falling back onto the bed. "Except for one little thing."

She glared at the brown-and-white rectangular sign boasting We Provide A High-Speed Internet Connection

For Our Guests' Convenience. She could run away from almost every source of frustration and fear in her life—but she couldn't hide.

She had no excuse now for not replying to Jacqui and Cydney. And worse, no excuse for not turning in her column. No excuse but the fact that she didn't have a column. That she had no idea what to say in a column.

"You have to take care of yourself and refill the well." She reminded herself of Lauren's excellent advice. Even Payt had told her she had to go after her dreams, to do whatever made her "happy happy."

And she had.

For about ten seconds when she came into this room she had been the most happy happy she'd been since…

"Since Tessa smiled at me last? Since Payt held me in his arms? Since I tucked Sam in bed thankful to God we'd had him for one more day?" Her daily life brimmed with happy moments—the sort of everyday ordinary happy that she had started to take for granted.

Or worse.

That she had pushed aside to make room for all the fear and worry that she fed with her own doubts and fault findings.

How had she let it go so far that the only way she could find to remedy it was to run away from her family and friends?

You know, sweet girl, insecurities and the driving desire for independence—they stem from the same place.

Hannah recalled Aunt Phiz's attempt to get her to confront the issue months ago. She hadn't had the time then, and wasn't sure even now that it would do any good.

It had been more than a year since she had stood at her mother's grave.

More than a year since she and her sisters had discovered the source of their mother's pain and chosen to forgive her even if they could not understand her.

How could they understand? Only her sister Sadie had been a mom then. Hannah and their oldest sister, April, had nothing to base their concepts of the mother/daughter bond on then. Just idealized visions, glimpses into the lives of their friends and the TV-show images that never wholly rang true.

But that had changed. With Tessa—and with Sam—that had all changed for Hannah. She knew now how much she could love another person, how much she could ache for them, how much she could sacrifice for them. And the toll all that could take on a person who didn't have a solid spiritual, mental and physical foundation.

Hannah's mom never had those things. Depression and circumstances had robbed her of them.

But Hannah had them and in amazing abundance, if she would just utilize them. She hadn't, and where had she ended up? In essence the same place her mother had—leaving her family.

Just that fast, in the time it took for her to think the very words…Hannah got it.

She got it.

Her mother's leaving had nothing to do with not loving Hannah. Or Daddy or Hannah's sisters. It had to do with not utilizing the abundance of help around her. In Mama's case, perhaps she simply could not do it, and even as it broke Hannah's heart to realize that, it also freed her heart to not just forgive her mother's actions but to love her.

"Wait. I did what my mother did?" A flush of panic shot through her body. She knew the fuzzy glow wouldn't last long in her. Gritting her teeth, she lunged for the phone.

"Bartlett Bachelor Pad, Soccer King speaking."

"Sam!"

"Hannah! I…I thought it was Hunter calling. Payt said he could come over tonight. And that we'd pitch a tent in the living room. And he—Hunter, that is—was supposed to call me as soon as his dad got home and could bring him over." Her kid didn't come up for air once until he gulped and tacked on, "Are you okay?"

"Yeah, *I'm* fine. I called to see how *you* are."

"We're all fine. You want to talk to—"

"I didn't ask about all of you. I asked if you are okay. I called to talk to *you,* Sam."

"You did?" His tone was hushed.

"Yes. I took off before you got home from school and didn't get to talk to you. I feel just rotten about that."

"That's okay. I expected you and Payt to be gone when I got out of school anyway."

"Is Payt taking it hard? My up and leaving on the vacation alone, I mean."

"I don't know. Want to ask him?"

"No! I don't want to talk to anyone else until I'm sure you and I are okay."

"Okay?"

"You know, like Hannah and Samuel."

"Yeah?"

"I think I can find a Bible in the drawer of the night-stand. Hold on." The wood groaned then pitched forward. Hannah had to lurch to keep it from plummeting to the floor, but she did and she found the Bible.

"How come you didn't take a Bible with you?" Sam asked as he waited.

"Because…" *Because I had fixated on the running away part of this adventure, not on the refilling the well part.* "Okay, here's the part I want to share with you. Are you listening?"

"Uh-huh."

"It's First Samuel, chapter one, verses twenty-seven and twenty-eight, if you want to, look it up for yourself while I'm gone and feel closer to me."

"Uh…okay."

You don't have to, she almost hurried to add. But she didn't. She let it go, satisfied that she had given him the idea and he might take some comfort in it. "Here's the verse. It's Hannah talking about her love and hopes for her Samuel. 'I prayed for this child, and the Lord has granted me what I asked of him. So now I give him to the Lord. For his whole life he will be given over to the Lord.' Do you understand that?"

"Not exactly."

"Yeah, it's kind of hard, I admit. For me, for us, it's a reminder that Hannah loved and wanted her Samuel, but that she knew that in their life they couldn't always be together."

"Like us." He said it so softly that she knew he was thinking beyond the five-day vacation to a time when their family might be torn apart by his biological father.

"Yes," she whispered. "But like us, Hannah knew that the Lord loved Samuel and would never forsake him. Sam, I love you and want you to understand that my going today was about me, not you. You didn't do anything to cause me to run away. And I am coming back."

"I know."

"Do you?"

"Sure. If it had been about me, you'd have called in my caseworker and I'd have gone to a shelter until my dad found someplace else for me to stay."

This kid understood rejection, the real thing, on a level that she never could.

"Besides, you left me with Aunt Phiz and Payt and Squirrelly Girl and Tessa."

"Aww, you couldn't put your baby sister before the dog?"

"Maybe when she starts talking and can say my name. That'll be cool."

"Yeah, that'll be cool." And Hannah would do everything within her power to make sure Sam stayed with them until Tessa not only said his name, but talked his ears off and beyond.

"Can I go now?" The whine of restlessness came through the line loud and clear. "As soon as Hunter comes over, we're going to pop popcorn and watch a movie."

"Popcorn?" She envisioned her plump stuffed frogs flatter than week-old roadkill. "What popcorn?"

"She wants to know what popcorn?" He didn't bother to cover the mouthpiece as he shouted out and got his reply. "Payt says to tell you no beanbag frogs were harmed in the making of this snack food."

"Very funny."

"You want to talk to him?"

"Depends. Is he willing to talk to me?"

Sam relayed the question. "He says 'always.'"

"Then tell him I don't need to talk to him right now. I still have to finish my column."

"Hey, good thing you have the Bible there. You can spend all night looking for the Book of Procrastinations."

"Go watch your movie, Sam. Love you."

"Yeah." And he hung up.

Hannah exhaled and stretched her legs out on the bed. Sam had been teasing her, but he did make a good point. She could, and probably should, spend the evening in the Word. But like too often in her life, she didn't have the time. She had to settle for a quick fix. She smoothed her fingers over the words of Hannah's prayer and muttered, "Peace. Be…"

It is not by strength that one prevails.

The simple line jumped from the page at her, and she hurried to turn the page back to the beginning of the segment.

"Do not keep talking so proudly…"

Listen to yourself, not everything is about you.

"…or let your mouth speak such arrogance."

"I write to communicate real problems of modern motherhood—silliness is not a part of it."

"For the Lord is a God who knows, and by Him deeds are weighed."

She closed the book slowly. "God knows and weighs my deeds."

Not Payt.

Not Lauren Faison, genuinely nice Supermom.

Not nameless letter writers or self-naming decorating sister duos.

Not even her minister.

Or her family.

"It's not my job to work for their approval but to be like Hannah who gave her beloved Samuel to the Lord. It's my life's work to never stop striving to become the woman God needs me to be."

She was needed, after all. Needed to be Hannah.

Wow. It all seemed so simple. Too simple, really.

Be the woman God needed her to be.

"But who is that, Lord?"

Wife?

Mother?

Daughter?

Sister?

Writer?

Volunteer?

"All of the above," she murmured as it dawned on her that it wasn't the role she chose or the work she did. It was the way she loved others—the way God wanted her to love them—that counted. The way she loved *them,* not how much—or even if—they loved her.

Thinking that made her feel so…stupid.

And corny.

And warm.

And happy.

Happy happy.

"I'm going to write that down."

You'll get a snotty letter about cornball platitudes, a little voice in her head warned her.

"Ha! You think I'm scared of that? I'm Moonie Shelnutt's daughter. What could anyone throw at me that would compare to crashing the Memorial Day Parade in Daddy's Caddy with my sisters a couple years ago? Or grabbing my bags and running away to Miami today?"

Oh, no.

That's when it hit her.

While Hannah's small rebellion might have helped her separate a mother's needs from a mother's love for her children, there was something more beneath the surface she had yet to address.

Yes, she forgave her mother and could now say she loved her despite a lifetime of questions. But the truth was, that looking over her life and the things that drove her day by day, the issues of her mother's depression and disappearance hardly ever came up.

Her issues had centered more on getting attention, getting approval. She had just wanted everyone to like her. Which sounded exactly like…

"Daddy!"

Daddy who acted like he didn't care what anybody thought of him, that's who she had struggled all her life to find in herself. Everybody liked her daddy. Even the people who wanted to wring his neck.

Hannah laughed softly.

All this time she'd grown so used to blaming her mother's leaving for her every fear and insecurity, but now…

Now she had run away from home, a truly Moonie-Shelnutt-worthy action if she ever saw one.

And like it or not, that lone act would become a part of her personal story. The day Hannah finally flew the coop!

"Might as well make the most of it." She took a deep breath and pulled her laptop from its case.

20

Subject: Nacho Mama's House column
To: Features@Wileyvillenews.com
Greetings from Miami! That's right—I'm sending out my column at the last minute, in the first hours of my pre-season vacation. I tell you that, not to engender sympathy, but because I feel the need to be totally honest.

At last.

Never in my days taking classes in journalism or my time managing the clinic in Wileyville or even in all my years of experience as Moonie Shelnutt's daughter did I ever imagine I would end up writing frank confessions. But here I am about to do just that. Those of you who have told me your secrets, don't sweat, though. Just send money and everything will conveniently be forgotten.

A joke. Am compelled to point that out. Ever since an anonymous letter writer went to great pains to let me know I am both too glib and not too witty, I find myself questioning every remark. Examining every turn of phrase for what might offend or confuse or simply fall short of the mark. Believe me, the supply is so plentiful that this act could very well take up what's left of my free time! I hope to work on that, on my writing, and do a better job of it in the future.

But then, that's the story of my life, isn't it? To step up to the plate, each and every time fearing I don't have what it takes, floundering, then afterward vowing I will do better next time.

And next time comes and...

Tonight I am in Miami curled up on a king-size bed in a beautiful hotel room that I had planned on sharing with my darling husband. But something came up at the office and he couldn't get away just now. He asked me to make a last-minute change in plans and I did. I came alone.

Yes, friends and readers, I have run away from home.

Or I tried to run away.

But it didn't take me long at all to discover that the things that drove me out the door, onto the expressway and through the barrage of airport bag scanners, drug sniffers, shoe examiners and all the other essential security measures of our time, were not things I could escape. You've heard of someone having a lot of personal baggage? Y'all, I have so much that if it had manifested itself in real trunks and suitcases we'd have never gotten off the ground. I could have walked to Florida faster than that poor overloaded plane could have flown.

But, since the only one who feels the weight of that kind of emotional baggage is the one carrying it, we made it here on time. And I started to unpack.

Not to press a metaphor too far, but the more I rummaged through the luggage of my life the more I realized I had been lugging around a lot of stuff I should have gotten rid of a long time ago. Worry, for one. And fear.

I guess to say "I worry a little" might sound to some of you like saying the Atlantic Ocean is a little damp. I worry all the time. I worry about my family. I worry about my work. I worry about my family's work.

And I worry about you, dear reader. I worry each and every time that I send off my column that you will read it and finally see the truth. That I'm a fraud.

Not fit to be published, for sure. Neither clever nor particularly insightful. Not as good as... You can fill in the blank, from your favorite syndicated columnist to your great-grandniece who writes you letters from North Dakota.

I am wholly, totally and woefully inadequate. Not just for newspaper writing but for so many things that I somehow have gotten myself stuck into.

Snack Mom. How can they stomach me?

Nursery Supervisor. I think I need crib notes!

Assistant Classroom Helper. More like Assistant? Classroom, help her.

Christmas Pageant Director. We Three Kings, Disoriented Are? Don't know why I got myself into this one and not sure how I will pull it off.

Uncompensated After-Hours Office Cleaner. At least for this one I am paid what I'm worth!

That was a joke, too.

Honestly, I don't mind cleaning in my husband's office, considering the work they do has so much meaning. The women who put in long hours there contribute so much to the health, happiness and welfare of others. I am in awe of them.

Just as I am in awe of so many women that I cross paths with during any given day.

The other soccer moms who practically live in their Mommy-vans but still find time to pitch in with schoolwork and bake homemade goodies.

The tireless volunteers at my church who, even though I sometimes make light of their foibles in my column, give freely of themselves with joy, creativity and boundless energy.

The neighbor lady willing to step in and help should I ever need her to remind me not to take myself so seriously.

My sisters who love me no matter what (not always an easy job), and who believed in me enough to submit my work before I even thought of it as work. They do so much: running a business, working for the city, maintaining a family and chasing after You-Know-Who (Daddy, do not go around telling people your youngest forgot your name). They are the cornerstones of both home and community.

And lastly, my Aunt Phiz, who flew all the way from India (not China) to come to my aid when she saw I had gotten myself into a hole and needed someone to hold up a light, show me the way and to pray for me.

You women inspire me.

You are amazing.

Delightful.

Strong.

Smart.

And a bit intimidating.

You are the reason I try so hard and why I take my failures even harder. I see all that you accomplish with your time, all you strive for, all you give, and am humbled at how often and in how many ways I cannot measure up.

You all are my heroes.

Not to slight the men in my life.

My minister, my father, my son and my husband have all shown extreme patience (except Daddy—on this score like daughters like father.) They have treated me with love, trust, goodwill and a colossal sense of humor. Really, for example, only a man who loved a good joke could have pegged me to direct the Christmas pageant after my inept handling of the nursery redo.

Each of these men has taught me something. I adore them all in different ways for it.

But let's get real, folks.

In the knock-down, brag-out, whiner-take-all brat-race of Mommies and Minivans, it's definitely a woman's world. For that I am grateful. The hand that rocks the cradle most definitely rocks!

It's been suggested to me by these remarkable women (and a few of the men) that I need to take the time now to listen, to learn, to laugh, to leave my fears and worries with the Lord.

It's not about outmothering the other moms, winning accolades or the desperate need to be liked at all costs. It's not about playing peacemaker or cakebaker or nursery wall-painter in the small hope someone will pat me on the head and tell me "Good job." It's about doing what a woman must do because she is called by God. I am called by God to love and be obedient to His will.

The prayer of Hannah, as evidenced in 1 Samuel 2:3, is still true today. "'Do not keep talking so proudly or let your mouth speak such arrogance, for the Lord is a God who knows and by Him deeds are weighed.'"

By Him my deeds will be weighed.

It's sound advice. I think I will take it, do my best and leave the rest with God.

Only thing left to do was hit send, then hit the hay.

21

Hannah couldn't recall when she had slept so soundly... or so late!

"Nine o'clock?" She forced her eyes to focus on the glowing green numbers a few inches from her pillow. That couldn't be right. She kept her alarm set for six-fifteen. Even so she never heard it go off. Tessa always woke up well before—

"Tessa!" She sat bolt upright, realizing she hadn't gotten up once in the night with the baby.

The crisp white sheets slid down to pool in her lap. Glorious sunlight streamed in through a wall-size window.

No coffee pot dripping. No Squirrelly Girl giving the low familiar *hooty-whoo* sound that the greyhound made to demand to be fed. No Aunt Phiz singing. No Payt showering. No Sam grumbling. No Tessa fussing. And when

Hannah got out of the bed, her feet would hit carpet, not scattered bits of dry cereal. Not slobber-covered dog toys. Not Payt's day-old discarded socks.

"I am definitely not in Loveland anymore, Toto." She stretched and savored the comparison to the storybook heroine who found herself transported to a magical, unfamiliar world.

"Where people bring breakfast right to your door," she said even as she picked up the phone and opened the room-service menu.

Fifteen minutes, they had said.

Everyone knew that in hotel-service speak that meant twenty, maybe even thirty minutes. More than enough time to grab a shower and read…

"The paper!" Her column. Last night after she had opened up her address book and hit send, she had put the thing out of her mind. But it was morning now, and time to face the music.

She just hoped it wasn't a funeral dirge for her career.

"You can do this, Hannah. You were honest with them. You should be able to handle them returning the favor." She drew in her breath, rifled through her makeup case for a hair scrunchie and padded barefoot to the small table where her laptop still sat open.

She settled into the sturdy little chair, brought her feet up and pulled her hair back. She caught a glimpse of herself in her laptop's blackened screen. With her once-sophisticated hair caught up in a ponytail, with no makeup and wearing pink pajamas with green cats on them, she looked all of twelve years old.

She felt all of twelve…and a hundred and twelve…all at once.

"Deep breath." She took one. "Turn on the computer." The machine hummed to life.

"And…connect." She pressed the button and waited.

"You've got—"

"Mayhem!" she said loud enough to drown out the cheery synthetic voice that usually greeted her when she checked her e-mail. "What is going on here?"

Screen name after screen name scrolled up one after the other, and not a one of them trying to sell a thing. It wasn't the number that staggered the mind, though, it was the names. Practically her whole address book accounted for.

And reading the headers, she instantly knew why.

Her fingers flew over the keys to help her confirm.

"I didn't." But of course she had. Physically worn-out from the trip, emotionally worn down from the events of the day, when she had opened her address book to send her column off to her editor, she clicked the wrong icon. She had accidentally sent her unedited, extemporaneous outpouring to everyone she knew.

And apparently most of them felt moved to respond.

One. That's the number of people she had prepared herself to hear from, the exact amount of criticism she considered ample for the piece she had submitted. "But now the whole world can tell me I am a dopey sap who should stick to writing about nachos."

Oh, goody.

"Better start with an easy one." She highlighted Sadie's address, but before she could open it, a rectangle popped up on her screen, accompanied by the pleasant little jingle of an instant message.

wlmom: Hey, Hannah! It's me, Lauren.

NachoMama: Hi.

wlmom: No time to chat. Just opened your fabulous e-mail and was trying to figure out when I'd have time to compose a deserving response.

NachoMama: Please don't trouble yourself. Sending out mass apology for the address book flub later today.

wlmom: Address flub?

NachoMama: Meant for eyes of *Wileyville Guardian News* editor only. Expected him to help me shape it up before anyone else saw it—if he even thought anyone else should see it. Yikes! Another Hannah-produced disaster.

wlmom: Stop that! I, for one, am pleased to have gotten the undiluted version.

NachoMama: Thanks.

wlmom: Want me to add you to my prayer list?

NachoMama: Sure, couldn't hurt.

wlmom: Enjoy the break.

NachoMama: Will try.

wlmom: Wait! Before I sign off—one question?

NachoMama: What?

wlmom: Where did you get the idea that the other soccer moms had time to bake?

NachoMama: The boys have bragged from day one that their mother's snacks were homemade.

wlmom: *LOL!* Hannah, Homemade is what everyone around here says when they mean they're from the Home Oven Bakery.

NachoMama: Store bought?

wlmom: A regional chain, no less. You can get the stuff at some groceries or at one of like, three or four locations.

NachoMama: <blush>

wlmom: There's one near the kids' school. Let's meet there one morning after we drop off the boys and talk over muffins and coffee.

NachoMama: That would be great. Now, can I ask you a question?

wlmom: Shoot.

NachoMama: Does your screen name stand for world's number one mom?

wlmom: LOL! Hannah, you're a hoot!

NachoMama: Thanks, I think.

wlmom: It's my initials—Wilma Lauren.

NachoMama: Wilma?

wlmom: World's number one mom! Where would you even get that?

NachoMama: Just guessing.

wlmom: Well, guess again. At least half of the time I feel exactly the way you said you felt in your column.

Everyone else seems so calm and cool and collected. Not me.

NachoMama: Thank you, Lauren.

wlmom: Thank you, Hannah, for starting my day off on such a thoughtful note. Am adding reading through the book of Samuel to my burgeoning to-do list! Bye.

NachoMama: Bye.

Lauren Faison felt just like her. Who would ever have imagined?

Sadie for one.

Loved it. Love you. Love yourself and see you when you get back.

April echoed the thoughts.

Aunt Phiz promised to stand by with prayer and light as long as Hannah needed her.

Hannah whizzed through those, but when she got to her minister's name, she paused. Had she insulted him with her crack about not knowing why he chose her? Would he dress her down for her flippant words?

Only one way to see.

Dear Hannah,
How you are going to handle the Christmas pageant? With style, girl! With style! And all the help you need. Just ask.

She smiled until it sprang to mind exactly the kind of help she'd gotten for her last church undertaking—the women poised and already waiting to help her right over the edge.

"DIYCyd has sent you an e-card." She searched and found the header easily. An e-card. From Cydney. "Hmm, wonder if she made it herself?"

If it were a do-it-yourself e-card, would it crash her computer? Hannah held her breath and clicked the blue link.

Doves and flowers and rainbows filled then faded from her screen while the computer dinked out the notes of "Wind Beneath My Wings." At last the words "You Are My Hero" swelled against a pink and orange sunset.

"Okay." Hannah waited for some kind of explanation, but the program ended with only the choices to view it again, respond to the sender or send the message to someone else.

"What message?" she asked the screen.

Click.

Back to her mail and the one, two, three e-mails from the other half of the duo. "Of course, Jacqui would have to outdo her sister."

E-mail one: Thank you,

E-mail two: Oops! Hit send with my charm bracelet. Thank you, Thank you, Th

E-mail three: Took my charm bracelet off. Maybe now I can get through a whole note.

Thank you, Hannah. Thank you a hundred times

over. You said it all. How I feel, and Cydney, we were on the phone to each other first thing this morning. You made it possible for me to tell you, and I speak— type?—for Cydney, too, our truth. We are miserable decorators.

"You don't say?" Hannah shut her eyes and shook her head to keep the images of the nursery suite incident from assailing her. After a moment she turned back to the e-mail.

We never wanted to decorate or design any- thing. Ever.

"Oh." She got it now. Jacqui wasn't confessing they made miserable decorators. They were miserable *because* they were decorators. That was her truth.

Gluing plastic gems to tennis shoes and putting up wallpaper borders in the guest powder room is one thing, but interior decorating as a business is beyond us. We just did it because people said we would be good at it.

"Really? Were these people drinking at the time?" Bad, Hannah. But she couldn't help it; knowing that the best mom in the world and the worst interior decorators shared the same insecurities that she did made her a little giddy.

We still want to do everything we can for the church and the nursery program.

"Giddiness subsiding," Hannah murmured.

So we thought why not take over child-care duties Sunday mornings? If we shared them between the three of us, we could all serve and still attend some of the services.

Hannah sat back, overwhelmed. That was the kind of help she could really use. The gift of time. "Wow."

She raised her hand to hit the reply button when a knock at the door drew her away.

"Room service!"

"Oh, breakfast!" She lost track of the time. So much for showering and getting dressed. She squirmed into her robe and grabbed her wallet to get some tip money. "Be right there."

She rushed to the door then, remembering a show she'd watched on the perils of travel, made use of the peephole in the center of the door. "Flowers?"

She couldn't get the door open fast enough. "I bet my husband sent these, didn't he?"

"I don't know, ma'am, I just deliver them."

"Oh, and breakfast—guess you didn't make that, either." She laughed.

He didn't. "No, ma'am."

"Um, okay, then." She stopped herself from launching into a lengthy story about how the misdirected newspaper column and the flood of empathy and support it had brought her had her unusually energized. Flashing her brightest I-am-really-not-a-nut smile, she pressed the tip into his hand and thanked him as she shut the door behind him.

The room filled with the aroma of bacon and roses, and instantly Hannah thought if they would ever make that a perfume, she'd buy it by the gallon. "They'd sell it by the gallon, too, in stores that sold everything for a dollar."

She left the breakfast tray on the dresser and set the roses down by her laptop. She took a deep whiff of the dark peach blooms, worked the small rectangular card free and murmured, "I am married to the most wonderful man in all of…Dr. Briggs's office?"

She blinked. Sure enough. Payt hadn't sent the roses— the women in Dr. Briggs's office had!

She read the succinct but very welcome message. "'We put a sign in the break room. 'Nacho Mama Doesn't Work Here Anymore. Clean Up After Yourself!' Enjoy your well-earned vacation.'"

More time. Wow, she wouldn't know what to do with it all. Starting with right now. Here she was all alone in a strange city in a strange state with no itinerary or plans. It was the kind of thing that sounded blissful in the midst of her usual chaos, but now she hardly knew what to do first.

Actually, that wasn't entirely true. She needed to make a phone call before she did anything more.

She sat at the table and dialed out even as she resumed opening e-mails.

The phone rang once, twice, three times, and she wondered if maybe they had all slept in when the one voice she wanted to hear most in the world answered.

"Bartlett here."

His voice warmed her to the center of her being. "Bartlett here, too."

"Good morning, sunshine."

"Well, the sun is shining in Miami, but how about where you are?"

"The weather is okay and so are we, though I might have heard the rumblings of low thunderclouds coming from Tessa's room."

"That's what you get for feeding her popcorn."

"It wasn't popcorn, it was canned chili."

She plunked her feet down so hard her chair squeaked. "What?"

"I was trying to improve on your nachos for the boys. Say, did you know that canned chili holds that can shape the entire length of time it takes to sail across the kitchen?"

She put her hand over her eyes. "I was going to ask if I should make plans to hurry home, but now I might just add an extra few days onto my stay."

"You can, you know."

"What can? We still talking chili here?"

"No. I think we're talking turkey. If that's what they call it when two people are speaking frankly."

"There's a bad pun in there someplace about turkey franks, I know."

"Hannah." His voice was deep and sincere.

"Payt?" Hers, more tentative.

"I'm sorry."

"*You're* sorry? I'm the one who ran away."

"No, you're the one who followed through on the plans we'd already agreed to. And I don't blame you."

"You should. I acted like such a baby."

"You acted like someone who was tired of always being a good soldier."

She knew how hard it was for him to bring up his childhood pain, and how genuinely he must understand her plight when he compared it to his own.

"I messed up the second honeymoon, Hannah. I made you work at the office and never told you how much I appreciated it. I do, you know."

"Yeah?"

"Yeah. No matter what, I always know you have my back, Hannah. You are the one person I always know will be there for me. I can't count on anyone—not my folks or brother or sisters—no one, like I can count on you."

"Always," she whispered, glad he couldn't see the tears puddling along her lashes. "Thank you for saying all that, Payt. You don't know how much it makes up for—the trip, the frustrations, the office. Oh, listen, speaking of the office—they sent me flowers."

"Lucky you, they sent me to the moon. Pow."

"Yeah, I can just see chubby gray-haired Dottie landing a wicked uppercut across your jaw." She trapped the phone against her shoulder and slapped her fist into her open palm for effect.

"She could have knocked me over with a feather when she called this morning to tell me Kaye agreed to fill in until we find a replacement for her."

She sat up so straight that the phone almost slid into her lap. She caught it in time to say into the mouthpiece without missing a beat, "Wow."

"Wow, and a few other choice words. Oh, they wanted me to make sure to tell you that none of them knew you were doing the cleaning, much less doing it for free."

"They didn't?"

"No. Wives working at the office is a very touchy subject ever since Mrs. Briggs died."

"I thought Dr. Briggs was divorced."

"The first Mrs. Briggs. She ran the office for nearly twenty years."

"Wow."

"When she died, Dr. Briggs had no idea what to do, and the first woman he hired took advantage of that—and him."

"Let me guess—the second Mrs. Briggs?"

"Yep. Anyway, that's what lay beneath so much of the turmoil in the office the past five years, and now that everything had gotten smoothed out…"

"You didn't want to risk more stress over wastebaskets and unwashed cups."

"Only, it didn't work. Kaye still quit and you got mad at me."

"And what have we learned from all this?" She laughed even as she asked it.

"Knock off trying to please everyone. Please God and He'll take care of the rest."

She wound around her finger a strand of hair that had come loose from her ponytail. "Was I too heavy-handed in the column with that?"

"I didn't think so. Have you heard from your editor?"

"Along with everyone else." She closed the e-mail from that very man and hugged one knee close to her chest. "He had a few suggestions and one very specific complaint."

"Yeah?"

"He wanted to know why his name didn't pop up in the men-I-adore-who-have-taught-me-so-much section."

"Figures." Payt chuckled, but just a little. "So what now, Hannah?"

"Well, I have to get on the rewrite and get it back to him. And there are a dozen e-mails here that need responses, and my bacon and eggs are getting cold."

"And after all that?"

"Do you need me to come home?" she asked softly.

"Absolutely."

"Okay."

"But not one minute before you need yourself to come home."

"Really?"

"Really. And what about when you get home?"

"I…I think I might go back to college and finish my degree. I have a lot to learn about writing."

"Great. And?"

"And I'd like for us start working toward getting your cousin to allow us to adopt Sam." She rested her elbows on the table.

"Long-range but, yes, I'm with you there. And?"

"And…I…uh…have decided I will direct the Christmas pageant."

"Should be great. And?"

"I don't know what you want to hear, Payt. That I'm going to quit writing? Because I really hope not to."

"I was thinking more in terms of starting something, not quitting."

"Oh, Payt. I'm just…" She pulled her legs up to her chest again and hunched her shoulders. "I'm not ready to have another baby."

"Are you ready to talk about it?"

"Yes." She unwound her body and set her feet on the floor again. "I can't promise that I'll have much to say. But I will listen."

"So will I."

"That's all I ever wanted."

"Me, too."

His tone conjured up an image of him as he must be this morning, rumpled and relaxed and a bit rough around the edges.

She sighed. "Wow, now I wish you were here with me."

"So do I."

"Then why aren't you?"

"A lot of reasons. One of them is that you took my plane ticket."

"No, I didn't. I worked it all out at the airport. You have a credit and can use the money toward a new ticket anytime you want."

"What about what *you* want? I thought you needed time alone."

"Give me twenty-four hours to unwind and catch up on my sleep."

"Are you asking me to fly away to you, Hannah?"

"I am, Bartlett."

"I love you."

"I love you, too."

"Twenty-four hours," he warned her.

"I'll be ready."

They hung up, and as she tackled the column rewrites and her first uninterrupted breakfast in a very long time, Hannah smiled to herself and thanked God for all the blessings in her life—even the ones that sometimes made her want to fly away.

* * * * *

Chapter One

❧

It's been said that when God closes a door, He opens a window.

Pretty handy, Sadie thought, if there's someone you want to push out of one.

Sadie Pickett was definitely in the pushing mood. Why not? She'd just seen all hope for the life she dreamed of dashed by the malice and greed of one man.

"Earl Lee Furst has got to go."

"Reach." Mary Tate McKrackin, her best friend in the entire world, didn't miss a beat. She met Sadie's gaze in the wall-sized mirror of the deserted-dance-studio-turned-charm-school, raised both arms over her head and asked, "How you plan to do it?"

"The only way possible." Sadie waved her hands half-heartedly over her head. She had only agreed to these after-hours exercise sessions because she'd thought *work-out* was a euphemism for getting *out* of the house and *working* her mouth by yakking and snacking.

Arms still extended, itty-bitty Mary Tate in her adorable exercise outfit bent at the waist. "You don't mean…?"

"You betcha." Sadie tugged up the band of the sweatpants she'd borrowed from her husband, Ed. A year ago she couldn't have gotten them on, much less moved around in them without splitting a seam. Today, she could fake a donkey-kick with the best of them and still maintain her dignity.

She bent and caught a glimpse of herself from the rear.

Such as it was.

"Yup, Mary Tate, that's my objective." Sadie ducked down low enough to peer under Mary Tate's arm. She wanted to get the full reaction when she unveiled her harebrained and highly improbable scheme for dealing with the man who had tested her good faith one too many times. "We're going to vote Earl Furst out of office."

Mary Tate bounced her body lower and lower toward the ground. "How?"

"How?" Sadie bounced right along.

Okay, she bobbed.

She bumped.

She outright bumbled.

Finally she simply bailed on the whole exercise scam and plunked herself down on the glossy hardwood floor. "I haven't figured out the 'how' part yet. But mark my words, the man is history in this town."

And he was, literally.

Like all the male descendents of the Furst family— Duke, Duke Junior, King, Noble, Little Noble and Mary

Tate's own husband, Royal—Earl's given name was meant to denote power and privilege. Unlike his uncles, cousins and the town-founding forefathers, Earl took this as a sign of personal sovereignty. He felt duly justified in that belief since the citizens of Wileyville, Kentucky, had elected him as their mayor an unprecedented thirteen times.

Thirteen.

That is one slow learning curve.

Or maybe no one else but Sadie noticed how the man never did any real work but still managed to grab credit for everything from a grade-schooler doing well in the spelling bee to the annual Tri-County Bass-travaganza Fishing Tourney. An event, by the way, where he personally cleaned up.

Profits, that is.

Not fish.

Maybe she alone saw that kind of thing and how, after so much time at the helm, Earl had gotten his fingers stuck into every aspect of life—and death—the town had to offer.

Sadie ran her fingertips over the words on the T-shirt her son had made for her: I Dig My Work.

It was not the worst pun she'd ever heard—or used—in regard to her position as the Parks and Recreation Supervisor/Superintendent of City Internment Locality. Sadie, a onetime Dogwood Blossom Queen, honors graduate of the University of Kentucky, mother of two, wife of the town's only pharmacist—and still able to send a baton twirling into air and catch it again without requiring medical assistance—had become the caretaker-in-chief of the town's living-impaired community.

She had Earl Furst to thank for that job and for the nick-name she'd earned because of it—"'Fraidy Sadie the Cemetery Lady."

'Fraidy because, well, it rhymed so well with *Sadie,* obviously. And because in her first few weeks on the job she had called the police a whopping ten times to come see about suspicious activities in or behind the graveyard. Uh-huh. *Ten.*

In a town this size word of *that* kind of dedication to one's job gets around.

The newspaper politely declined to do a story.

The police stopped taking her calls.

Folks in general suspected her daddy, Moonie Shelnutt, was behind the mischief as he was so much of what went awry around town.

Mayor Earl Furst had even wormed his way into the hospital where Sadie and her sisters had rushed Moonie after what looked like a small stroke. Under the guise of concerned public servant, he had wasted no time in reminding Sadie that many, many people would like a job where they were not expected to do anything and *she* had better start not doing anything herself...or else.

No, he didn't say "or else." But he did make it clear he wanted her to work less and ask fewer questions.

She compromised. She worked as much as she saw fit and kept her mouth closed—sort of. But you can believe she kept her eyes open.

The high jinks subsided in time. Or maybe she just became accustomed to lights and sounds at odd hours. To things in her office going missing. And to the heavy machinery, tons of mulch and dirt and the few sundry supplies stockpiled in the storage area shifting around over the course of a night.

That's how it was around here. People became accustomed to all manner of things they knew weren't quite right or that they couldn't quite explain and went about their business. They took for granted that the people they elected would always work for the best interest of the town, and if something seemed amiss, it was only because they—the citizens—didn't see the big picture.

Folks in Wileyville were definitely small-picture type of people. Because of this her father could derive the maximum amount of attention for a minimum amount of eccentric effort—marching with the toddlers in the Memorial Day parade or driving through town on a riding lawn mower while wearing a Statue of Liberty headpiece kept town tongues wagging for months. That suited him just fine. But while Moonie Shelnutt thrived on that small-picture mind-set, Mayor Furst counted on it.

That's how he was able to pull off his betrayal of Sadie and Ed. After a year of dinners, development deals with the town council and something called due diligence, where men in ties and rolled-up shirtsleeves examined everything but Ed's undergarments, they had been lulled into a sense of assuredness that the sale of their business would go through. Then one eleventh-hour decision by the mayor put the kibosh on the whole arrangement.

Sadie wriggled her fingers along her scalp to loosen the pull from her lopsided ponytail. A strand of hair fell across her eyes, and instinctively she searched for any gray mixed in with the reddish-brown. "I just can't believe he did this to us."

"Believe it, girl." Mary Tate whooshed a long blast of air through her lips and took a moment to grab one of the towels she'd kept draped over the ballet barre.

No one had stood at that barre for a bona fide ballet class in years. Pilates, cheerleading, kickboxing and co-tillion now kept the doors of the Royal Academy of Charm and Beauty open. At least until Mary Tate got the no-tion—and enough extra money in her business account—to up and have the sign on the window repainted. Then maybe she'd add martial arts weaponry and Bible-based meditation to the list. Who knew? The girl who had once rescued Sadie from death by high school gym class had grown into a woman with a knack for always trying new things. That and a gift for never completely giving up on the old.

She'd never given up on Sadie. That was for sure.

"How could anything Earl does surprise you?" Mary Tate dropped her bottom to the floor and faced Sadie. "The man has run this town for more than half our life-times."

Sadie grinned and lounged back on both elbows. "Our *real* lifetimes or the substantially shorter lifetime you *claim* to have lived?"

"Hey, I have documentation for that claim." Mary Tate nudged Sadie's feet out until she could press the pristine white treads of her athletic shoes to the flimsy soles of Sadie's sneakers. Arms out, Mary Tate wriggled her French-manicured fingers.

"Yeah, yeah, your parents put the wrong year on your birth announcements." Sadie slapped her hands into her friend's. "But your birth certificate tells another tale."

"Yes, but no one has seen that certificate in years, whereas my birth announcement…" She jerked her head toward the wall covered in framed awards, citations and photographs of winning dance troops.

"Vanity, thy name is Martha Tatum Fitts McKrackin."

"Do not start bandying about Christian names, Sadelia Nellie Shelnutt Pickett."

"Point taken." Sadie shuddered at hearing her full name spoken aloud. "I was just teasing you, you know. I don't think you're *that* vain."

"And I don't think you're *completely* nuts for this idea of yours."

"Just this much nuts?" Sadie held up her hand, her thumb and index finger a hairbreadth apart.

Mary Tate mimicked the gesture, widening the gap.

They clasped hands again and began the gentle preliminary give-and-take of angling backward just enough to pull the other person's upper body into the space created by their outstretched legs, then reversing the movement. A warm-up before the full-body torture, Sadie liked to think of it.

"I can't help it, Mary Tate." Sadie shut her eyes. The tight knots in the small of her back eased slightly as her friend's weight dragged her forward. "I just want…"

Her voice cracked.

She cleared her throat.

She pressed her lips together. Tears stung her eyes but didn't fall.

"What, honey? What do you want?" Mary Tate whispered.

She couldn't say. She really could not say. Not because she didn't know. She wanted now what she had always wanted.

She wanted her husband of twenty years to look at her the way he did two decades ago. She wanted him to cherish her, or at least notice when she was or was not in the room. She wanted her teenaged children to come to her for more than borrowing car keys and credit cards.

She wanted to accomplish things. She wanted to become a force to be reckoned with. She wanted more than anything to know that when her life was over, God and the people she loved would say, "Well done, thou good and faithful servant."

She wanted to know that what she did mattered.

"What, Sadie? What do you want?"

"What I want…what I *don't* want…" She looked up and straight into the loving eyes of her oldest friend. "I don't want to be a loser."

"Sadie! Honey, you were never that. This isn't the depression talking is it?"

Sadie shook her head. It had taken time, medical attention and the help of a Christian counselor she still saw once in a while, but she had moved past that dark time when depression had ruled her life. "I do thank you for asking, though. People refusing to talk about it never helped a thing."

Mary Tate nodded, the space between her perfectly plucked eyebrows pleated with concern.

"Maybe *loser* is too strong a word." Sadie took a deep breath and started another round of slow warm-up stretches. "I just wish that for once all my following the rules, being a team player, trying my best to do what's right, having faith in others and keeping my eyes on the prize would pay off."

"Oh." Her friend's forehead smoothed. She rolled her eyes. "Is *that* all?"

"Tall order, I know. But I am so tired of seeing people like Earl Furst, who don't do any of those things, win all the time. Mary Tate, I want to know what that feels like. Just once in my life I want to win."

"You aren't thinking of running against Furst for mayor, are you?"

"Me! No! Never!" Sadie could hardly swallow for the rush of panic the very suggestion triggered in her. Run for office? Her? It was ludicrous. "No. No, I just want to be on the winning *side*."

"Then call Furst Campaign headquarters, I'm sure they'll give you all the buttons and yard signs you can handle."

"Not *that* winning side."

"It's the only one in town, honey. No way will anyone around here mount a viable campaign to defeat Furst."

"Defeat Furst. I like it. How's this for a slogan?" She let go of her friend and made a sweeping gesture with her hands. "Sadie The Cemetery Lady Says Let's Get Earl Out Of Office—Defeat Furst."

"Hmm." Mary Tate crooked her fingers to silently draw Sadie back on task.

Sadie obliged. "Get it? Cemetery lady? Feet first?"

"Oh, I got it. And for future reference, hon, just because I don't laugh at your graveyard humor doesn't mean I don't understand it."

Sadie stuck out her tongue.

Mary Tate responded in kind, then cocked her head. "Did you come here to exercise your body or your jaw?"

"Jaw," Sadie shot back.

"Too bad. Hang on." Mary Tate leaned back.

Every muscle in Sadie's body stretched. Hard. She groaned.

"You are so out of shape," her friend taunted.

"Does the flattery ever stop with you?" Sadie wrinkled her nose and took her turn leaning back. "Isn't it bad enough you think I'm nuts for thinking we need a new mayor?"

"The man is not just *a* mayor, Sadie, he is *the* mayor. That means he can do as he pleases. Including not budging on the concessions that national chain demanded of the city before they'd buy this place out."

"Technically they aren't buying *this* place out."

Technically they were clearing Ed out of the way so that they could dominate the market. They would buy his stock, his records, access to his contacts and his promise not to compete against them. They had no interest in the old, triangular-shaped building on the wedge-shaped piece of land at the easternmost end of Wileyville. The building that also housed the Royal Academy, the place of business everyone had called Picket's on the Point for twenty-four years, would be vacated.

"Okay, let's really go for the burn this time." Mary Tate scootched her bottom in like she was hunkering down to boat a marlin.

Sadie took a vicelike grip on her friend's hands. "If only…"

"Don't waste your breath on 'If only.'" She pushed her feet flat against Sadie's and made every effort to flatten her back to the cold floor.

Sadie protested with a very ladylike "Ugh."

It only egged her friend to pull harder. "Besides if someone *did* run against him and Earl won anyway, which he would, he'd just point to that as proof that he can do whatever he wants around here because he has the voters' mandate."

"*Man*date," Sadie managed to mumble with her face pressed to the floor. "*Man* being the operative word."

Her friend sat up straight in a slow, controlled movement. "More like the good old *boys* network that keeps him in power."

Sadie broke free to rub her cheek then braced herself to give as good as she got. "Too bad us good old girls don't have a little network of our own."

"Yeah, too bad. Not that it would matter. Earl's been serving—"

"Ha!" Sadie leaned back with all her might.

Mary Tate pitched forward.

"Earl Furst has not *served* Wileyville in years, and you know it, Mary Tate. Wileyville has served him." Sadie let go of her friend's hands. And right there on the floor of the Royal Academy, 'Fraidy Sadie the Cemetery Lady made up her mind. "And I, for one, think it's about time that changed."

Discussion Questions

1) Hannah notes that in modern American motherhood not all the competition is limited to the soccer field. If you are a mother, have you ever felt a sense that you were competing with other mothers? How did you handle it? In what ways can we, as women, become more supportive of, and less competitive with, each other?

2) Hannah often found herself at odds with the people who thought they were helping but in truth created more work for her. Eventually, by being honest with them and by seeing them as people who had their own issues and emotions not unlike hers, she found a new appreciation of them. Do you have people like this in your life? How do you handle them?

3) Hannah uses e-mail to keep in touch with her family and as a link to her work. Do you think the Internet has helped you to form closer bonds? How so?

4) For at least the first two-thirds of the book, Payt was cute but clueless. He eventually came around, at least to some degree. Was that realistic? Do you think men are fairly and realistically portrayed in women's fiction? Should they be more or less realistically shown?

5) Hannah made a journey from someone who followed the verse she had been raised on (from Daniel 10:19— "Peace. Be strong.") to 1 Samuel 2:3 ("Do not keep talking so proudly or let your mouth speak such arrogance, for the LORD is a God who knows, and by Him deeds are weighed."). Do you find you draw strength from different verses of the Bible at one stage of your life, then grow into others? Do you have a chosen verse that you rely on in troubling times? What is it and how does it help you?

6) All the characters in *Mom Over Miami* are people who rely on faith to help them make decisions. Can you see that faith at work in the decisions of Hannah? Aunt Phiz? The DIY Sisters? Payt?

7) As a writer, Hannah receives a critical letter that confirms her worst feelings and fears about herself. Have you had times when others made you feel this way with the nature of their criticism? How did you deal with it?

8) Hannah resorts to a drastic but harmless measure to get the attention of her husband and family. Do you think most moms have had moments like this? Do you think it's appropriate for a mom to sometimes shake things up in order to let the family know they are taking her for granted? If you are a mother now, did becoming a mom change the way you looked at your own mother?

9) If you could run away from home today, where would you go? How do you think your family would react? What do you think you might gain from such an experience?

10) Does considering the actions of fictional characters help people gain a new understanding of themselves and others? In what ways do you think fiction can help people in their daily lives?

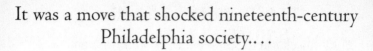
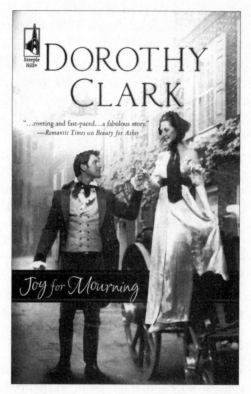

From *USA TODAY* bestselling author Deborah Bedford comes BLESSING

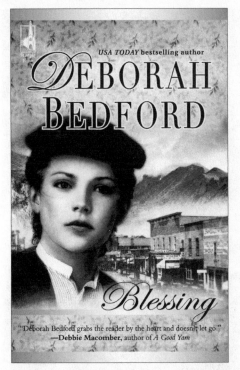

The secret beneath Uley Kirkland's cap and mining togs is unsuspected in 1880s Tin Cup, Colorado. She longs to hide the clothing of deception and be honest about her feelings for handsome stranger Aaron Brown. But while Uley dreams of being fitted for a wedding gown, the man she loves is being fitted for a hangman's noose, and she is the inadvertent cause of his troubles.

The truth will set them free, and Uley will do whatever it takes to save Aaron's life—even risk her own.

Steeple Hill®

It was a story to put Hideaway, Missouri, in the national headlines…

CHRISTY AWARD-WINNING AUTHOR

HANNAH ALEXANDER

"…CROSSOVER APPEAL TO FANS OF MEDICAL SUSPENSE AND OF SUCH AUTHORS AS TESS GERRITSEN."
— *LIBRARY JOURNAL*

Last Resort
A Hideaway Novel

A missing child…
A woman in crisis…
A man of faith…

Don't miss this next exciting novel in the Hideaway series.

In stores June 2005.
Visit your local bookseller.

Steeple Hill®